Tempting Prudence

Book 2, The Bride Train

E.E. BURKE

Tempting Prudence is a work of fiction. Names, characters, places and incidents are the product of the author's imagination or are used fictitiously.

Cover Design by Erin Dameron-Hill
Train photography by Matthew Malkiewicz
Digital formatting by Author E.M.S.

Published by E.E. Burke
ISBN-13: 978-0-9969822-9-0

Author's Note

The Bride Train was inspired by a series of true events that took place in southeastern Kansas shortly after the Civil War. When the government opened former Indian land for settlement, the railroads used their political power to purchase large tracts. Settlers who'd staked claims under preemption rights were forced to broker deals with the railroads.

By 1869, riots broke out in protest of railroad land policies. Angry settlers burned ties and tore up track as fast as the railroad could put it down. As the situation worsened, President Grant sent troops into Kansas to quell the violence.

A more peaceful solution was proposed: a program sponsoring the immigration of single young ladies into Kansas to become brides and provide a "calming influence" on the unruly men. I couldn't find evidence this program got off the ground, but what a great romance series idea!

Why did I choose to write about a bootlegger? Genealogy research revealed that family members on my husband's tree were involved in the illegal whiskey trade back in mid 1800s. The character of Arch Childers is loosely based on stories about those enterprising ancestors.

In 1862, Congress passed a law making distilling liquor without a license a federal offense (mostly because the government needed tax money to pay for an expensive war). Thus was born the illegal distilling industry and the long history of American *moonshiners* and *bootleggers*.

The term *moonshine* originated in Europe and originally referred to occupational pursuits that necessitated night work, or work by the light of the moon. Moonshiners worked at night so the smoke from their stills couldn't be seen. The term *Bootlegger* is believed to have originated in colonial America in reference to those who sold alcohol to Native Americans. The practice was frowned on (for many reasons I won't go into here), but some more determined peddlers wanting to trade spirits for material goods concealed bottles in the top of their boots. The terms are often used interchangeably, but strictly speaking, the *moonshiner* manufactured the illegal whiskey and the *bootlegger* transported and distributed it.

In the West, illegal stills became the source of running battles between moonshiners and law enforcement officials who sought to shut them down. To avoid detection, stills were often located in remote mountainous areas with thick forests, like the Missouri Ozarks. This is where my character hails from, and where my husband's ancestors hid their stills.

I hope you enjoy *Tempting Prudence*.

– E.E. Burke

Dedication

*This book is dedicated to
my husband's enterprising ancestors.*

Prologue

Taken from an advertisement posted by the Missouri River, Fort Scott & Gulf Railroad in Eastern U.S. newspapers:

EVE, FIND YOUR ADAM
IN THE GARDEN OF THE WORLD!

Single young ladies of good reputation desiring to emigrate west for the purpose of marriage may apply to the Young Ladies Immigration Society for free travel to southeastern Kansas, where hardworking settlers are eager to make their acquaintance and become steadfast husbands. Applicants must be free to wed, of marriageable age, preferably between the ages of 18 and 25, without deformities, debts or other encumbrances. Dance hall girls, circus performers and soiled doves need not apply. Must provide references.

From a letter dated April 8, 1870, written by Mrs. A. Langford, president of the Young Ladies Immigration Society and honorable member of the MRFS&G Railroad Board of Directors, to Mr. R. Hardt, newly hired land agent in Cherokee County, in regard to the success of the society's matrimonial efforts:

The first bride train arrived in Girard, Kansas, on March 15. These young women, all of them respectable ladies, remained single for no more than a week. They have already had a calming influence on the unrest in Crawford County. We anticipate the same effect will be felt in Cherokee County subsequent to the delivery of more young women who are able to meet the men's matrimonial needs.

However, you must be aware the arrival of the prospective brides did not stop the Land League from stirring up trouble. The insufferable rebels are worse than an infestation of rattlesnakes and used our rally as a distraction. Whilst some men bid for picnic baskets, others slithered off to burn railroad ties. Our loss was catastrophic. Beware, lest the same thing happen to you. The sooner matches are arranged the better.

Rest assured, the railroad's board remains committed to this program, which will have its intended effect. Facilitating marriage isn't solely a benefit to the railroad. It is for the good of the country. Lawlessness and savagery will not have the last word! The West will be settled, one bride at a time.

Chapter One

May 24, 1870,
Centralia Settlement, Southeastern Kansas

Prudence Walker possessed neither beauty nor a sweet nature. Facts she had accepted long ago. She had in her favor a strict upbringing, which had kept her from straying off the narrow path and had taught her the value of diligence in all things, including cooking.

"He becometh poor that dealeth with a slack hand: but the hand of the diligent maketh rich." She quoted one of her father's favorite proverbs, as she gave the potatoes another good whisking to ensure the fluffy texture her mother had insisted on.

If an eligible bachelor showed up at the Lagonda House for the noontime meal, she might snag a husband today. She certainly hoped so. That's why she'd taken the train west, to the end of the line. This was her last chance at matrimony.

Having reached the mature age of thirty unmarried,

she wouldn't hold out hope if she weren't in a place where men outnumbered women ten to one. The odds had encouraged her to answer a railroad advertisement seeking respectable young women willing to immigrate to southeastern Kansas for the purpose of marriage.

The ad hadn't mentioned that the majority of available men were uncouth, given to violence and indulged in all manner of vices.

Prudence chose to believe that out there somewhere was a *Daniel*—a God-fearing, peaceable, temperate man—in need of a likeminded wife. Maybe today she would meet him.

She draped a checkered cloth over the bowl to the keep the potatoes warm and checked on the chicken sizzling in a cast iron frying pan on top of a black box stove. There were worse places to be alone than in a well-appointed kitchen. Transferring the fried chicken to a china platter, she set it on the worktable next to the mashed potatoes and snap-peas. Soon, the bread would be ready.

Laughter drifted in from the dining room. Her friend Hope peeked around the door. "Are you still cooking?"

"I'll be finished soon." Prudence allowed she would finish sooner if she had help. Thus far, her friends hadn't offered. In all fairness, she hadn't asked for help, either. The other ladies, who had also arrived on the Bride Train, had picked up different chores in return for room and board. Not an ideal arrangement, but it would only be temporary. Soon, their prayers would be answered and they would find suitable husbands.

"We're walking down to the mercantile to see Mr. Appleton's selection of hair ribbons." Hope brushed a fringe of mahogany curls off her forehead. She could use a few ribbons. Her hair coiled every which-way, resisting all efforts to tame it. Oddly enough, Hope didn't seem to care that her hair misbehaved.

"Do come with us, Prudence!" Delilah appeared over Hope's shoulder. Her saucy black curls were created with a hot iron and pulled back with decorative combs. Prudence admired the style, but she would never wear something that would make her appear vain. She was content to braid her hair into a coronet or pull it back into a brown snood the same color as her hair.

"Thank you for asking me along. I don't need any ribbons."

"I'll find you a pretty one, anyway," Hope promised. "And we'll be back in time to help you serve dinner."

"Thank you, I'd appreciate that."

A yeasty smell filled the kitchen as Prudence pulled two pans out of the oven. Placing the loaves on their sides, she covered the warm bread with a cloth to keep the crusts soft. She loved baking bread, from preparing the spongy dough to kneading it smooth to removing a fresh baked loaf. Some found the process tedious, but making bread gave her satisfaction. The kitchen had always been the place she felt most comfortable. In here, she didn't need to be beautiful or desirable. She only had to be competent.

A loud banging came from the back door. Another delivery. As summer approached, more farmers were arriving in town with fresh fruits and vegetables. One of them might turn out to be the kind of man she hoped to marry.

She removed the soiled apron and smoothed her skirt. She'd worn the serviceable gray wool, knowing she would be working in the kitchen. If she had time, she would change into the brown calico for dinner. Pausing by a small mirror mounted on the wall near the back, she checked to make sure there was no flour on her face. Wouldn't be the first time.

Solemn brown eyes gazed back at her. Would the

caller find her attractive? Her nose was straight, but a tad too large to be considered classic. Her upper lip looked thin compared to an absurdly full lower lip. Her brother had teased her when they were children, pointing out her perpetual pout. Her odd mouth would be less noticeable if her chin were less square.

Rapid banging jolted her out of her daze. Good thing whoever it was hadn't given up and left. She would've missed her chance to meet him. That's what came from being overly concerned with her appearance. No wonder her father had prohibited mirrors except for the small ones on washstands.

She opened the door with what she hoped was a winsome smile.

Three men stood at the bottom of the few steps leading out to the back yard. Cookie cutter replicas of many of the Western men she'd encountered: unkempt and unshaven, wearing dusty denims and scuffed boots and felt hats with brims that flopped over their eyes.

Prudence hid her disappointment behind a polite smile. "May I help you?"

The tallest man, whose coal black beard reached his chest, tugged his hat brim. "Mornin' miss, um…"

Politeness required they make introductions first, but the men out here seemed to care little for good manners.

"Walker," Prudence supplied.

"Miss Walker. Right. You're one of them women who came to town on the Bride Train. I ain't too good with names."

She happened to be very good with names, and faces, and she couldn't recall seeing these three in town and was certain she hadn't taken deliveries from them.

"Yes, I arrived on the train…" Prudence glanced past them at a wagon hitched behind two mules, which didn't appear to be loaded with anything, save a coffin. Her heart grew heavy at the memory of two pine boxes in the back of her brother's wagon. Were the men on their way to bury a deceased relative? "My condolences for your loss."

"Yes ma'am, thank you…" The youngest looking of the three, a gangly, ginger-haired fellow with bright red whiskers, held his hat in his hands. "We thought we might find a kind woman like yourself who's willing to help…"

The purpose for their visit became obvious. Possibly, the men had spent the last of their money on a coffin and couldn't afford to pay for dinner. She hadn't prepared for extra mouths to feed. Yet, she'd never turned away someone who was hungry. The guests could make do with one loaf, and a few pieces of fried chicken wouldn't be missed. Prudence glanced over her shoulder. No one had come into the kitchen, so she wouldn't be seen giving away food.

"Wait here. I'll get you something to eat."

"No ma'am, we don't need a handout." The younger man reached out. If he stood closer, he might've grabbed her skirt. "All we need is your help. We got a hurt pup."

"An injured dog?" Prudence's heart went out to the poor creature. Caesar, their family's sheepdog, had been her dearest companion. Losing him had broken her heart. "What happened? Did the dog tangle with a snake? Or was it a wagon? People drive too carelessly, just yesterday, I was nearly run down…"

She closed the door and set out for the wagon with the men trailing, so close she could smell the tobacco smoke that clung to their clothes and the unpleasant odor of stale sweat. Thank goodness they weren't suitors. She had no desire to curl up beside a husband who smelled worse than his horse.

The third man, who'd been silent, moved up next to her. His bulky shoulders and heavy brow reminded her of her uncle's bulldog. Her heart sped up. She disliked being boxed in. He seemed oblivious to the impropriety, and appeared more worried than ill tempered.

"I was raised on a farm, so I have some experience with nursing animals," she assured him. "Where is the poor thing?"

"Show her," the bearded man's command came over her shoulder, making her nerves jump.

The bulky man grumbled under his breath as he shifted the coffin lid to one side.

Startled, Prudence took an abrupt step backwards, bumping into the tallest man's chest. Flustered, she moved forward and peered into the coffin.

No corpse. No dog. A sick joke, that's all it was, and this wasn't the first time she'd fallen for mean-spirited foolishness. When she'd been fourteen, the leader of the boys at school had put a dead cat in a box and presented it to her as a gift.

She turned on the freckle-faced man, who'd withdrawn a large blue handkerchief from inside his coat. "This isn't funny, if that's what you think. There is no injured dog, is there?"

"Sure there is…" The young man's tone rang with sincerity, almost convincing her that she'd misjudged. "And you're gonna get to meet him."

Unease lifted the short hairs on the back of Prudence's neck a split second before the bearded man behind her locked a beefy arm around her neck.

A wadded handkerchief cut off her scream.

The coffin lid slammed shut.

Prudence's shrieks came out muffled. One of the

devils had gagged her, while the other two bound her wrists and ankles. They'd tossed her, struggling, into the pine box, sealed it and then sped away.

The wagon lurched and hopped, bouncing her up and down.

She writhed, twisted her wrists and kicked her bound legs, winced at every bruising jolt. No matter how hard she struggled, she couldn't free herself. She was at the mercy of three men who thought nothing of stealing a woman. What kind of creatures would do that? Where were they taking her? What would they do with her once they reached their destination? The likely outcome was too horrible to consider.

Prudence bit down on the cloth, grinding with her teeth. That didn't work, either. What should she do? What *could* she do?

Pray without ceasing. That's what her father would've advised.

"Our Father who art in heaven, hallowed be thy name, thy kingdom come thy will be done..." Her heart thrashed in her chest like a trapped bird beating its wings against glass. The sound reverberated in her ears, drowning out her ability to think. She couldn't recall the rest of the prayer. *Thy will be done...will be done...will be done..."*

No! This couldn't be God's will.

She labored to breathe as her chest grew tight and her throat closed. Nothing happened outside the Lord's will. Her father declared this from the pulpit with absolute certainty. He'd never wavered in his beliefs, never weakened...not like her.

Maybe the Almighty was angry with her. The Lord knew she longed for a husband and children. She wouldn't be satisfied to remain single and miserably alone, even if that was His will. *Forgive us our trespasses... Forgive me...*

The wagon dropped, and her breath left her lungs as the coffin lifted into the air. As abruptly, the pine box slammed down. Her shoulder struck one side, the pain barely registering before she was flung to the other side and treated to the same punishment.

A thud, followed by creaking wood, indicated someone sat on the lid. Muted curses were followed by low laughter. How could humans be so heartless? Maybe they weren't human. Angels had visited earth. Why not demons?

Fear slammed into her with the force of a tidal wave, dragging her under...suffocating her... Her racing heart felt nigh unto bursting.

Calm down. Take slow breaths. Don't pant like a dog. Above all, keep your wits about you.

She had weathered other storms—the horror and grief when her best friend had drowned, the anguish over the loss of a beau who'd died in the war, a disastrous wedding, the loss of both parents within days of each other. She could make it through this crisis if she regained her composure and used her head for something besides a hat rack.

First, assess the surroundings.

A gleam of light shone through a pencil-sized hole above her feet. In her panic, she hadn't seen it before. So, they hadn't planned on smothering her, but they had planned on abducting her. What had they asked? If she was one of the women who'd arrived on the train. That meant they were after one of the brides. Had they singled her out? The thought that they had been watching her made her skin crawl.

Whoever they were, whatever the reason for their bizarre behavior, they were up to no good.

If she could draw attention... She hammered the side of the coffin with her heels. Someone pounded on the lid, followed by more laughter. The noises drowned in the rattle and rumble of wheels rolling over rough ground.

"Nobody saw…got clean away…"

Prudence strained to hear the muted conversation. Got away to where? The town, such as it was, ended at the hotel. From there, the road led south. At a fork, the road veered southeast and followed the railroad tracks. Another path curved west and ended at the edge of the vast grassland. Trapped, with limited use of her senses, she had no way of knowing which direction they'd gone.

Her continued attempts to draw attention by kicking the coffin were ignored.

The wagon rolled on for what seemed like an eternity.

Perspiration poured from her skin and soaked her undergarments. She grew parched. The sun had turned the pine box into a sweltering oven and being unable to move about had made her limbs lose feeling. Her arms were the first and then her legs. Numbness spread like an insidious disease. Even her mind grew numb. Was this what it felt like to die?

Her parents spoke of their lives passing before their eyes. Prudence imagined a whirling zoetrope like one she'd seen at the fair. Hers didn't feature colorful, exotic images. Every picture remained the same. Dull. Unremarkable. Uninteresting, like her. The decision to immigrate west and marry a virtual stranger had been the most exciting thing she'd ever done. It might turn out to be the last thing she ever did.

Her brother had scoffed at her decision to be a "railroad bride." Enoch's frowning face—angular, severe, so like her father's—invaded her mind.

"You disappoint me, Sis. What do you think you'll find in Kansas? I'll tell you what: rioters, drunkards, outlaws and savages. Take heed. Forming alliances with disreputable men will result in a lifetime of sorrow."

Enoch had quoted their father to make her doubt the wisdom of her plan. She knew her place in God's order, but she couldn't bring herself to bow to her eldest brother's decrees. His arrogance rubbed against her pride.

Yet, he'd put his arm around her shoulder and concern had warmed his brown eyes, a feature they'd both inherited from their mother. Father's eyes had been the clear, cold gray of a winter morning.

"You'd be better off coming with us to California..."

Much as she hated to admit it, Enoch had been right. If she'd gone with him and his family, she wouldn't be in this fix. Better unhappy and alive than adventurous and dead.

A shudder racked her body and then another. She didn't want to die. She wanted to live. If God would save her, she would never do anything imprudent again.

"Whoa!" The driver's call interrupted her misery. She tensed as the wagon rolled to a stop.

Whoever sat atop the coffin moved and the lid was lifted off.

Prudence blinked. A flash of blue sky, a scowling, bearded face...and then she was hauled out of the coffin, passed from one set of rough hands to the next. Her limbs hung numb and useless. She could resist no more than a rag doll.

The bearded giant grabbed her hair, tore off the snood and fished out the hairpins. Gagged, she moaned in protest as her unbound hair tumbled down her back and into her face.

"That's better," he muttered. "Now get her loose."

The burly man untied the binding around her ankles and released her wrists. She couldn't feel her hands and feet and would've collapsed had someone not been holding her up.

"We don't need this no more," said the ginger-haired

accomplice as he untied the gag. "You can scream all you want, nobody to hear you...except us.

Scream? She couldn't produce a sound through her dry throat.

The wagon had come to a stop in a clearing about a stone's throw from a small dwelling sided with unpainted clapboard that might've been shipped in by rail. Beside the open doorway, a red coonhound barked. The timbered area behind the house would indicate the presence of water, possibly a stream. Railroad tracks were laid near water, weren't they?

She frantically scanned the landscape, praying she would recognize something, a landmark, anything that might help her find her way back after she managed to escape.

The sun hung low in the sky. That direction was west, and out there was nothing but a sea of tall grass, undulating like waves.

She had no idea where she might be, or which way she ought to run, or if she could run.

Feeling returned to her limbs with a vengeance, she flexed her fingers to speed the painful process. Her rubbery legs threatened to give way. She didn't have the strength to wrench away from the bearded man's grip; was at the mercy of three brigands whose plans seemed abundantly clear. They'd brought her to this lonely place to ravish her and would likely kill her afterwards.

The air smelled fresh, like newly mown hay. But being able to breathe freely didn't calm the sick churning in her stomach. Weakened, unable to hold back the nausea, she leaned over and vomited on the trampled grass.

With a grimace, the skinny abductor held out the handkerchief he'd used to gag her. "You almost got my shoes."

13

"Won't make you smell any worse," cracked the bearded man, who held her arms fast.

If he released her, she would run. Even if she fell on her face, it was better than accepting her fate.

The shorter, heavyset man ambled toward the cabin. "Arch! Git out here…we brung you a present."

Dear God. They planned on passing her around?

A man's figure darkened the doorway. His shoulders filled the framed-in entrance. Her heart accelerated as he emerged, half-dressed, his chest bare as a savage's. Suspenders dangled on either side of his legs from the waistband of worn denims. He threaded his fingers through shoulder-length hair the color of a tarnished penny and stared at her with a fierce scowl.

Prudence tasted fear. The metallic essence that filled her mouth also seemed to permeate her bones and muscles, rendering her paralyzed. Four strapping males, and this last one appeared to be half-wild. How could she hope to fight, or escape? She was doomed.

The man behind her tightened his grip, keeping her upright, holding her out like a prize. "Come meet yore new bride!"

Chapter Two

What the Sam Hill had his worthless brothers done now?

Arch made the distance between the house and the sagging woman in Obadiah's arms in less than six long strides. "Are you *crazy?* What the devil…"

Before he could formulate words to express his outrage, his eldest brother shoved the bedraggled female at him. He had to move fast in order to catch her before she folded up like a loose-jointed puppet. He got his arms around her ribcage and hauled up her up against him in an awkward embrace.

The boneless doll jerked up straight as a soldier. With a terrified screech, she went at him with her fingers curled into talons. He dodged a sweeping assault, barely missed getting his eyes gouged out, and had to snatch her wrists to stop the attack.

"Sheath your claws, gal! I ain't gonna hurt you."

His brothers jerked out of their startled trance and lunged at them.

"Keep away!" Arch's bellow halted them in their tracks. By God, he'd kill the misbegotten curs for

15

frightening this poor woman. They'd scared her so bad she'd lost her mind.

He held her by her wrists at arm's length and danced side-to-side to evade her kicks. Growing desperate, he dragged the little wildcat up against his chest again, pinning her arms to her sides, tight enough that she couldn't get her hands free, but not so tight he'd injure or suffocate her.

"Whoa now, don't fight me! You're safe. Nobody's hurt y— Ow!"

She'd nailed his shin with the toe of her shoe. He winced and sidestepped. "Calm down." He used a firm, but kind tone, and continued shushing her, crooning into her hair, assuring her he'd keep her safe.

Almost as fast as she'd changed into a feral cat, she went back to being a limp doll. "Please," she begged in a pitiful, hoarse voice. "Don't a-abuse me…" Her voice wavered and she sagged in his arms. Her shoulders shook as she sobbed silently.

Her distress fanned the flames of his anger until it was hotter than a blacksmith's furnace.

He raised his eyes, pinning a hard look on each of his brothers. Obe stroked his long beard and didn't flinch. Vernon Lee and T.J. looked away, acting oblivious.

"Get out of here. Now." Arch snarled the command.

Amusement glinted in his eldest brother's eyes. "Don't be gettin' your dander up, bub. We done you a favor by bringing you this woman. They'd all be gone by the time you got around to courtin' one, and then where would you be? Without a wife, you cain't secure your land. The way I see it, you ought to be thankin' us."

Obe's decisions were frequently rash, but this crazy act made the other stunts he'd pulled look like child's play. This time, he'd find himself at the end of a rope— and the rest of them alongside him.

Arch spoke through clenched teeth. "I'll thank you with a load of buckshot in your backside."

The humor in Obe's gaze vanished and his expression flattened. "You need a lesson in respect little brother."

"Yeah, well, we can teach him later." Vern put his bulk in front of Obe and held him back with ham-sized hands. "We ought to leave now, so they can get acquainted."

Arch supposed he should be grateful to Vern for playing peacemaker, although part of him longed to have it out. He wasn't the weakling Obe thought he was.

The woman in his arms shuddered. Her loose hair concealed part of her face so it was hard to see what she looked like. A glimpse revealed ashen skin and haunted dark eyes.

Arch kept her enfolded to make it clear she was under his protection. Not something that was likely to soothe her, but he wanted her to know that she would be safe from harm as long as he drew breath.

"We didn't hurt her. Just tied her up and brought her to you. Didn't even use rope." T.J. held up several long strips of plaid cloth, looked like from an old shirt.

So tempting to take those cloth bonds and wring T.J.'s scrawny neck.

"Are you so stupid you don't realize the damage you've done?" Arch fumed. "Look at her. She's so scared she can't talk. Might not be in her right mind after this."

T.J. rubbed at a thatch of red bristles, as if the thought hadn't occurred to him that he might've done the woman permanent harm. He wasn't callous, like Obe, but he didn't think for himself, followed their older brother's lead. "She'll come out of it after we're gone."

"You better hope so."

"Time to go…" Vern wrapped a heavily muscled arm

around T.J.'s bony shoulders. He clapped his hand on Obe's broad back. "We can celebrate a wedding—without the bride and groom."

The three of them fought like spurred roosters one minute and hugged each other the next. They had always been inseparable. Growing up, Arch hadn't been part of the tightknit circle, no matter how hard he'd tried to fit in. Now, he wished they would leave him alone.

Obe threw him a final look that said he'd be back to settle things. He had a foul temper and any slight would set him off. Arch didn't care if he'd angered his brother. Wouldn't be the first time. The two of them had never gotten along.

As the ornery cusses retreated in the creaking wagon, Arch curled his fingers around the woman's waist. She wasn't tiny, but she had nice curves and full hips. Not that he ought to care about her hips, or any other part of her.

He couldn't imagine what insanity had possessed his brothers to steal a woman, and a plain one at that. Maybe they intended it as a joke. Wasn't a bit funny. "My brothers are idiots, but don't worry, they won't hurt you."

What a stupid thing to say. They'd manhandled her, injured her pride, her reputation, quite possibly, her mind. He could say he was sorry, but an apology was far from what she was owed.

"If you'd like, I'll be happy to thrash 'em. Have to do it separately, or I'll end up trussed and hanging upside down from a tree branch. They did that to me once. I got them back, though. Put ants in their boots."

His attempt at levity was met with a dull gaze. She wasn't in a humorous mood, and he ought to know better than to make light of a harrowing situation, regardless.

He couldn't imagine where they'd found her. The

rumpled gray dress looked more suited to a prim old lady, but her rich dark hair didn't have a speck of gray, and it tumbled over her shoulders past her waist. The women he knew who wore their hair down were prostitutes.

Regardless, she was a woman and had been put through a hellish experience. Could be she needed a doctor. He'd send for his ma if it came to that, the fewer folks who knew about this the better. "Let's go inside, sit for a spell. I'll get you some cool water."

Her head came up, fresh terror flooded her face; she shook off whatever weakness had taken hold and pulled away, backed up a few feet and faced him on shaky legs. "I'm not going in there with you."

Nothing he'd done would've given her the idea that he would take her by force. He heaved a patient sigh. "Look here, if I wanted to hurt you, I could've done it by now."

She kept on hugging her arms while shooting arrows with her eyes. "Return me to Centralia. Immediately. If you don't, I swear I'll see you hang."

Unease skittered over his skin. A whore would probably ask for money.

Arch raised his hands, palms out, in a peaceable gesture. "Easy now. No need to get me in trouble."

"If you don't take me back…" She clutched the skirt, lifting the hem like she was prepared to run. Her slender wrists were marked with abrasions, probably from twisting her hands trying to escape her bonds. God knows what story she would tell. Didn't matter. Folks would take one look at her and assume she'd been violated. The soldiers assigned to keep the peace would take him to jail, and his brothers along with him—unless a lynch mob got to them first.

He had to stall, find out her name, make sure she wasn't hurt worse than what it appeared. "I'll take you back…after I clean up those scratches on your wrists."

She dropped the skirt and looked at her arms, appearing surprised. That confirmed her mind wasn't working right if she hadn't noticed the injuries. Those had to be painful.

"Why don't you tell me your name?" He considered not giving her his name, but she'd heard his brothers use it, and if she described him, any man in town could give her his identity. "I'm Arch. Short for Archer, but you can call me Arch."

Her ghostly cheeks turned rosy as she stared, wide-eyed, directly at his chest.

He glanced down. *Shoot.* He'd forgotten he hadn't put on a shirt. Now it made sense why she thought he would drag her inside and molest her. "I, uh, wasn't expecting company, was washing up. Shaving. I'll put on a shirt when we get inside—"

"Prudence Walker." She averted her eyes, and used her fingers to comb tangles out of her hair. Her hands trembled. "They-they took my hairpins…and my snood."

That pretty well cinched it. The curs had snatched a lady, not a whore.

"I'll get your things," he vowed. He'd take a pound of flesh along with it.

She peered up at him through thick lashes. With her hair combed out of the way, he could see her face better. Tear-streaked and a little dirty, but not as plain as he'd first thought. Her dark, luminous eyes reminded him of an alert doe. "After you take me back…"

Her plea tugged at his heart. He knew the longer he continued to stall the more upset she might become, but she was already shaking hard and she'd be even worse off after being jostled around for another hour on a bumpy road. "Miss Walker, I fully intend to take you back. But you look like you're about to drop. I know I'd feel better if you would come inside and sit down. Maybe take some tea."

He motioned for her to go ahead of him into the house.

She shook her head.

"All right then. If you won't go in, I'll bring a chair out to you." He slipped inside and grabbed two chairs tucked up under the table. Once he got her situated, he'd see to getting her something to drink. Whatever it took to convince her not to report him and his brothers, he'd do it. They couldn't afford another run-in with the law.

He stepped outside.

She'd taken off. Lit out in the direction of the creek.

"Wait!" He set the chairs down and took off after her. What was the fool woman thinking to hotfoot it down a steep, rocky path? "That's not the way back to town."

She ran faster—though he was sure she'd heard him. Her long hair fluttered behind her like a ragged banner. If she didn't watch out, she'd trip over one of those sycamore roots.

Suddenly, she stumbled. Her legs got tangled in her skirts and down she went. Hard. Skidding to a stop, she lay crumpled. Still.

He dropped to his knees next to her, his heart pounding so hard he could hear it. Should've known the poor woman was unbalanced and not to let her out of his sight. "Dang it all to perdition."

Being gentle as possible, he turned her into his arms.

Her chest moved. Breathing, thank God.

He brushed the tangled hair out of her face. Her smooth skin had turned as white as one of those porcelain dolls he'd seen in the window of the mercantile. Blood ran freely out of a cut along the edge of her scalp.

Carefully lifting her, he cradled her limp body and started up the path as fast as he could go without stumbling or losing his grip. He had to get her to the house and staunch the bleeding. The cut would need to be stitched. When she woke, she'd have a devil of a headache and would have to stay in bed for a few days, maybe a week, and he'd thought he was in trouble before. Now, he had an even bigger problem on his hands.

Something damp laved her face. A wet tongue…odiferous breath… "Stop bathing me, Caesar," Prudence mumbled. She raised her hands to ward off the eager licking. When the dog wouldn't stop, she turned her head.

A sharp pain made her gasp. Someone had embedded a knife in her forehead.

Moaning, she forced her eyelids to open a crack. A black nose appeared, sniffing her face. Loose skin hung from the dog's snout. So it wasn't a sheepdog, and definitely not Caesar. Where had the hound come from, and why was it on her bed? Why did her head pound as though it would fall off? Her eyes drifted shut as the questions melted into awful memories…or were they dreams?

She remembered being in a coffin. Buried alive. Bearded men leered at her and tossed her bound and gagged, to and fro, cackling like demons. Someone lifted her into strong arms that formed a safe cradle. She snuggled against what felt like a solid wall and could hear inside a heavy *thump, thump, thump*.

A low voice whispered in an unfamiliar drawl. "*Hush now, be still. I won't leave you.*"

"Git down, Rebel!"

The harsh command startled Prudence out of the troubled, half-sleep. She snapped her eyes open in time to see a flash of fur as the dog leapt off the bed.

A man's face, wreathed in auburn hair, hovered over her. His heavy russet brows drew down over eyes as blue as a bright summer sky. The bridge of his nose had a slight bump, suggesting it might've been broken at one time. A slight cleft softened an otherwise square chin. His lips were thin, or maybe it looked that way because he had them pressed together. She didn't know him. Yet, he looked familiar…her dream rescuer?

Dazed and not sure she wasn't asleep, she spoke. "Why are you in my bedroom?"

His eyes widened with surprise. He parted his lips as if he might say something, but then closed his mouth and gave her a crooked half-smile, which transformed his features into a compelling blend of flirtatious boy and rugged man.

He twisted away. She followed his movements as he pulled a straight-back chair over to the side of the bed. "You got conked on the head pretty hard. I hear that can rattle your memory."

Her gaze wandered to the ceiling and she frowned, confused. The hotel didn't have rough-hewn timbers or a clapboard roof…and this place had an earthy smell, like a root cellar.

A rush of memories blew away the fog that had settled over her mind. The coffin, the three devils abducting her, she hadn't dreamed the nightmare, it had really happened.

Alarmed, she tried to sit up.

The world went spinning.

"Whoa, slow down." The auburn haired man—he was the one who'd chased after her—caught her arms, preventing her from rising. She didn't have the strength to fight him, and her head rang like the inside of a church bell.

With a groan, she slumped onto the pillow. So soft, it had to be down. "Goose feathers," she murmured.

He patted her shoulder. "*Horsefeathers*, you mean. Yep, it is awful frustrating when you can't sit up without the room whirling. But you got to rest. Give yourself a chance to heal. That cut bled like the dickens, took five stitches."

"Cut? Stitches?" This explained the roaring headache.

"You don't remember?" Sitting back in the chair, he rested his hands on his knees. His knuckles bore numerous white scars and the tip of the little finger on his right hand was missing. In addition to that bump on the bridge of his nose, a thin white scar slashed through his right eyebrow making it appeared raised. He looked as battered as the old tomcat that had lived in the barn. Even his unruly hair reminded her of the cat's reddish fur.

Thank heavens he'd donned a shirt. Though the memory of his muscular chest was tattooed on her brain. How was it she could recall the patch of brown hair over his breastbone and his hard pectoral muscles when she couldn't remember striking her head?

She lifted her hand to assess the damage to her forehead.

He caught her wrist. "Don't pull off the bandage. It took me two tries to get it wrapped right."

"What happened?"

"My brothers brought you here."

She shuddered. "I remember that part."

He leaned forward, seeming to search her eyes. "Do you recall me telling you it was all a big mistake? I tried to get you to sit down and rest, but you ran off, down the path to the creek. Tripped on a root, hit your head and cracked it open... I had to doctor you through a fever. You talked crazy for a couple days. Your fever broke last night."

His voice hinted at weariness and the signs of strain were visible around his mouth and eyes. Maybe he'd thought she would die and he would be blamed for it. Or he might've dreaded having to find a place to dispose of her body. Although, if he wanted her dead, or simply wanted to use her for sport, he wouldn't have brought her into his home and tended her.

At a troubling thought, she slipped her hand beneath the covers. She wore nothing but her thin shift. He'd even removed her drawers. Horrified, she pulled the quilt to her chin. "You...you undressed me."

No leer or smirk crossed his face. "Had to," he said, matter-of-fact. "You were bleeding all over your clothes, and I couldn't bathe you down fully dressed."

The thought of him removing her clothes, those large, scarred hands on her body, did strange things to her insides. Her skin heated as if the fever had returned. She didn't dare mention it. He might try to bathe her again.

"You feelin' poorly?" He leaned forward, reached out to feel her forehead. The faded blue cambric shirt pulled across his shoulders and bunched up around the suspenders.

She stared, mesmerized, unable to forget what he looked like without the shirt. His virile body stirred hungers she never knew she had.

A warm, calloused palm made contact with her cheek and the quivers intensified; spread like wildfire across her body, making her skin prickle and her breasts peak. His touch should appall her. She shouldn't feel all hot and shivery, and heaven forbid, excited.

Prudence screwed her eyes shut, praying he couldn't see how his touch affected her. This had to be some odd reaction that came about as a result of his intimate care when she was senseless. She couldn't be attracted to the heathen. His evil brothers had abducted her. Then he'd balked when she asked him to be returned. She couldn't imagine what he intended to do with her, but she wasn't staying around to find out.

Somehow, she had to get away. How would she manage when she couldn't lift her head more than a few inches off the pillow, much less stand without toppling over?

She heard sloshing water and then a damp cloth covered her forehead and eyes. The coolness absorbed some of the heat on her face and eased the throbbing headache.

"Relax now. You'll feel better quicker if you don't fight it." He brushed his fingers over her temples, so gentle it seemed like he was stroking her hair. Her mind had gone for sure if she mistook simple compassion for sweet affection. He had no tender feelings toward her. More likely, he presumed she would welcome him into bed if he petted her.

"You have a dog," she murmured, reaching down to a warm indentation in the quilt. Thank goodness. That wasn't her imagination. She felt safer with the animal between them.

"You met him. Rebel. He's been curled up next to you for two days."

Two days. She had been here *two* days.

"Has anyone…come by?"

"No." He didn't offer an explanation.

Who would care, really, if she simply vanished off the face of the earth? Oh, her friends might ask around, but then what? They'd assume she had up and gone home because she hadn't found a man to her liking.

Her lips quivered and her eyes began to burn. She reached up and put her hand on the cloth, holding it in place, swallowed to rid her throat of the wad of misery stuck there. Wallowing in self-pity would get her nowhere.

The man whistled. Something landed with a thud on the bed. She reached down without looking. The dog licked her fingers then stretched out and wriggled up next to her, trying to get as close as possible. She stroked a smooth head and floppy ears. The pup scrabbled closer, and with a loud sniff, laid its head on her chest.

Her tension eased, and she smiled. "Thank you."

"My pleasure," the man replied.

"I was talking to the dog."

She heard a soft chuckle.

"You and Rebel get acquainted. I'll get you something to eat." He made it sound so natural, as if he was used to having her around and getting her meals, waiting on her. She'd taken care of people all her life, but couldn't recall anyone ever taking care of her. She could learn to enjoy the attention.

Gadswoons. What nonsense.

Prudence removed the cloth from her forehead. It was past time to come out of hiding and find out what kind of predicament she'd landed in. Moving slowly, so as not to jar her aching head, she came up on her elbows and scooted into a sitting position. She held the quilt to remain covered.

A gray blanket nailed to overhead beams formed a partition between the sleeping area and the other side of the cabin. The privacy curtain made her feel marginally safer. Beyond the chair positioned by the bed was a washstand with a chamber pot.

She remembered a little more from her dreams...something she'd rather forget. A man had assisted her with personal acts she hadn't let her mother help with since she was a girl.

Now, she was in her right mind and had no intention of allowing him continued liberties. She would ask him to return her dress and escort her to town.

"Mr. Archer?"

The dog's head came up. His tongue lolled and he thumped his tail on the quilt. When he stretched out, she could see that one of his back legs was severed at the knee. Part of an ear was missing, as if some animal had taken a bite. The dog must've tangled with a larger creature and come out on the losing end.

She scratched behind Rebel's scarred ear. "You look like a war veteran. Is that why he calls you Rebel?" Or it could mean his owner had Confederate sympathies.

Mr. Archer didn't look within five years of thirty, which meant he'd been a youth when the war broke out. That wouldn't have stopped him from joining the fighting. Mere boys had lied about their age and signed up on both sides.

Rustling sounds came from the room on the other side of the blanket. He must not have heard her the first time she called.

"Hello? Mr. Archer?"

After a moment, the blanket drew back and her host entered the cramped space, carrying a steaming ceramic mug. An unpleasant aroma filled the air. "You hungry? Got some soup here. Marrowbone. It'll build your strength. My Ma swears by it."

He ordered the dog off the bed and handed her the cup.

She'd prepared a strengthening broth from bone marrow for her parents when they were ailing, but this soup smelled like dirty water. "Thank you, but I think I'm strong enough."

"Go on. It tastes all right. You need to eat something."

Using one arm to hold the quilt so she wouldn't expose herself, she returned the mug to its owner.

"Thank you, but no. If you could bring me my clothes, I'll get dressed and you can take me back to town. There's plenty to eat at the hotel."

He sat in the chair and leaned to one side to put the mug down. She peeked over the edge of the bed. A deer hide partially covered the packed earth floor. Beside the bed was a bucket filled with water.

"Miss Walker? We need to talk." He appeared more solemn than he had been up to this point.

"About what?" She rubbed her aching temple. Her head would likely throb for days.

"Your head hurts."

"Is that what you wanted to talk about?"

"No. But if your head is hurting, you won't be in any mood to talk." Reaching into his back pocket, he withdrew a small medicine bottle and popped off the cork, held it out to her. "Here, have a swig."

Her former betrothed had carried on his person a flask of liquor, although he had insisted it was for medicinal purposes.

"If you're offering me liquor, I'm not interested."

He waggled the bottle. "It's a tonic my Ma makes for headaches. From a plant the Indians call *the five-fingered friend*. You'll see why when your head starts feeling better."

Prudence took the bottle and sniffed. Smelled of herbs. Doctors prescribed tonics all the time, so how bad could it be? Considering her head felt like a split pumpkin, she might as well try his mother's home remedy to see if it would help.

She took a timid sip…slightly bitter, but not horrible. Tipping the bottle, she drank more. Before she could down another swallow, he swiped the container out of her hand.

"Go easy. That's strong medicine."

She did feel a slight rush of warmth, although the

throbbing didn't subside. "What did you say your mother called it?"

"Headache tonic." He corked the bottle and returned it to his back pocket, watching her with an expectant expression.

"When will it work?"

"Soon."

"Maybe the headache will go away after you find my clothes."

He braced his hands on his knees and pinned her with those piercing blue eyes. A jolt of excitement bounced from the top of her head all the way down to her toes. Did he experience the same reaction? If so, his face didn't give anything away.

"There's no need for you to wrestle into a dress. You aren't goin' anywhere. You got to stay in bed and rest. I'd say, a week."

"A week?" She hugged the quilt, incredulous. Her head hurt, granted, but she wasn't so frail she needed to be coddled. Sick or not, staying here alone with a man who wasn't her husband or a family member was out of the question. "I'm sure I'll be well enough to travel. After I get dressed."

"Miss Walker…" His solemn expression sent a chill down her spine. "You'll need to stay in bed at least another week, or you risk falling ill again. Being a well-bred lady, you know how it'll look with you disappearing and being out here with me for so long…alone."

"Of course I know what people will think, which is why I need to go back. Now. No one needs to know," she added in a low tone.

She would be glad to keep her mouth shut and tell no one about her shame. Except, his brothers might decide to snatch another unsuspecting woman, so she had to warn her friends.

He regarded her steadily. "Hard to keep something like this a secret. The way I see it, there's only one thing we can do."

A shiver passed through her. Despite the warmth of the air, her skin grew chilled. "What...what's that?"

"We got to get married."

Chapter Three

Prudence gaped at the madman. "You're as insane as your brothers, Mr. Archer."

The intensity burning in his extraordinary eyes flickered out as if her reply had doused the flames. His back grew as straight as the chair and his features took on a stillness that indicated she'd offended him. "Childers, that's my surname, Miss Walker. Archer is my given name. But everybody calls me Arch."

She had gotten his name wrong, and insulted him. Despite the absurdity of his proposal and whatever motive had prompted it, she had no cause to be rude, and especially in light of how well he had cared for her. The fault had to be this headache—that, and her fearful situation. "I apologize, Mr. Childers."

"No apology needed. Reckon I didn't make my name clear enough."

"I'm apologizing for calling you insane."

"You offended me more by comparing me to my brothers."

Prudence searched his eyes. Amusement lurked in the blue depths. He was back to teasing her, which must be his way of dealing with a tense situation. After seeing him get so angry, she worried he might have a bad temper. Good thing he was more duck than bear—as her grandfather would've said—letting things roll off his back rather than taking a grudge into hibernation. "Only in one way did I seek to make a comparison—your sanity. I grant I might've been mistaken in that."

"Good to hear you make mistakes. A perfect woman can be tedious." The side of his mouth lifted in a crooked smile, prompting a flutter in her chest.

"I'm far from perfect, I assure you..." Ah, this provided a way to refuse him without implying he was lacking in some way. "In fact, you'd find me a very poor wife. Stubborn. Opinionated. Difficult to please..." She listed her worst qualities. "One day you'll thank me for refusing you."

His steady regard didn't waver. The way he looked at her, as if he could see through her, made her nerves jump. Though her head felt better.

Prudence touched her temple. Indeed, the throbbing had lessened and her stomach didn't pitch anymore. "Why, I believe your mother's tonic helped..."

"Good. Now you need something to eat. If you can't stomach that soup, how about biscuits?" He stood. Apparently her refusal didn't upset him overmuch. He hadn't demanded an explanation or attempted to change her mind. For some reason, this annoyed her.

"You do understand why I can't marry you..."

He paused in front of the hanging blanket. "I understand why you might not be ready to accept my proposal, but we'll get there..."

Her mouth dropped open at the same time he dropped the curtain behind him. He intended to hold her here until she came around? He couldn't truly mean to go through with it. Or maybe he did, and that's why his brothers had abducted her. There were too many men, not enough women, so why not steal one? Only an immoral man could come up with that kind of logic.

Prudence threw back the covers and swung her legs over the side of the bed.

The ropes beneath the feather mattress creaked.

She froze, waiting, half expecting him to come storming back and order her to bed. He might use force to stop her from leaving.

From the other side of the curtain came the sound of whistling.

Dixie.

Hearing that song made her skin crawl. Prudence put her hands over her ears. No dyed-in-the-wool Confederate for her, and he had to be a democrat. She made a face. Another reason she wouldn't marry him— as if she needed another reason.

Taking advantage of the continued noise behind the curtain, she braced her hands and inched forward, sliding until her feet touched the dirt floor. The room didn't spin thank heavens. A wad of cotton inside her head remained, which was a feeling that would soon pass. After being in bed for two days, she ought to expect her mind would be fuzzy.

She didn't see her dress. He'd left his coat hanging on the back of the chair. She shrugged on the garment, which swallowed her in its bulk. Buttoned up, it would cover her, if not decently. She'd worry about decency after she escaped.

He started banging pots...or was he cooking? He'd gone to a great deal of trouble for her. That didn't mean she was obligated to marry the odd fellow, and certainly not if she had to listen to him whistle that infernal tune.

She tiptoed to a window with greased paper covering the panes, which wasn't uncommon out here. Actual windows were rare, glass even more so. Arch's roughhewn cabin looked to be more permanent than some of the lean-tos and tarpaper structures dotting the countryside, which had been built solely to satisfy claim requirements. The land rush in Kansas had become famous for attracting fortune hunters. Arch might intend to stay, rather than sell out before the ink dried on his deed. She wished him luck. In spite of everything, he'd done her a good turn by tending her while she was sick. She wasn't about to remain here, however. Not for another day, much less a week.

Her stomach let out a growl so loud he would've heard it had he not been making such a racket. He'd started singing. A rich baritone that was far more pleasing than the whistling. Pity he didn't know another song.

Prudence managed to raise the window sash without noise. If she carried the chair over, she could climb out the window. Thank God he kept singing.

The awkward exit ended with her falling out the window and landing in a bed of soft dirt, on top of something that gave way. Something damp and squishy...smelled like...melon.

Scrambling to her feet, she brushed off the dirt and sticky residue. She hated messing up his garden, and his coat, but there was no time to fix her mess. There would be time later to clean his coat before returning it.

His garden backed up to a pasture. Standing there with its head over the split rail fence was the largest horse she'd ever seen. The dapple-gray shook a luxurious white mane.

Prudence's spirits lifted. She'd get away faster if she could coax the beast into letting her ride. That would mean stealing. *No, borrowing.* She would return the horse along with the coat.

"Hello there, beautiful girl." Prudence moved closer. She checked to be sure she hadn't insulted the horse. Indeed, a mare.

The gray's ears perked forward, indicating curiosity. Having lived on a farm, Prudence knew how to approach a strange horse. No quick movements that might startle the animal. The mare allowed a few strokes on her velvety nose before wandering away to nip at some fresh grass.

Prudence found a halter at the gate and lured the mare using an immature carrot she'd ripped out of the soil. Desperation had reduced her to vandalism and thievery.

After haltering the horse and forming reins using the lead rope, she brought the mare to the fence. Within a couple tries, she managed to climb to the top rail and get her leg over the horse's broad back. She pulled down her shift and rearranged the oversized coat, so she wasn't sitting bare-assed astride the horse. Flushed with excitement and a sense of imminent victory, she picked up the rein, patted the horse's neck, and touched her heels to its sides.

The mare plodded dutifully through the open gate.

Oh joy! She'd done it! Escaped, whilst her captor whistled *Dixie*.

How she wished her over-bearing brother could be here to see. He wouldn't be so dismissive of her ability to get along on her own. He had never acknowledged her abilities, even though she'd cared for her ailing parents with no help at all.

Prudence headed across the clearing, away from the grassy prairie. That way led to Indians. Town would be east. She would keep to the path. Doubts niggled the back of her mind: she might get lost, or she might run across someone less honorable than the rascal who saw nothing wrong with abducting a bride...

Loud barking came from behind.

Dash it. The dog had spotted her and sounded the alarm. Using her heels, she urged the horse into a lumbering trot.

A shrill whistle pierced the air.

The horse came to a jarring halt.

Unprepared, Prudence lurched forward. She flew over the horse's withers and slammed into the dirt on her back. Her breath lodged beneath her breastbone. For a moment she couldn't make her lungs work.

Rebel stuck his nose in her face, sniffing. The traitor.

"Pru!" The shout sounded surprisingly close, and the thundering steps, which didn't come from hooves. The addlepated mare stood motionless, looking down at her with not a bit of remorse in those luminous orbs.

"You all right?" Arch knelt beside her. His anxious frown registered a second before she made the connection. *The whistle.* That's what had stopped the horse.

She closed her eyes, groaning. Curse him for training the horse. Curse the horse for learning.

The beast bent its massive head, nuzzling her hair in an apparent plea for forgiveness.

"It's too late for that," Prudence muttered.

"Git back, Sophie." Arch grasped the rope dangling from the halter and pulled the horse away. A few soft words, a gentle pat, and the shameless hussy trotted right back into the pasture.

"Here, let me help you." His voice dropped low, taking on a soothing tone.

"Don't talk to me like that. I'm not as easily led as that mindless horse." Prudence pushed at him when he scooped her into his arms. She might as well try to push a boulder. To her utter humiliation, she began to cry. The fall had shaken her confidence, the pounding headache had returned, and the blasted dizziness.

He lifted her with ease like she was petite and delicate, rather than a sturdy woman who was too plain and too old for him to possibly want. She fought an urge to wrap her arms around his neck, to be as complacent and willing as that monstrous nag.

Acting as if he didn't notice her weepy eyes and red nose, he cradled her against his chest and headed back toward the house. "You're lucky Sophie didn't buck you off. She don't like strangers riding her, and she's so broad she's hard to sit bareback. You stayed on her pretty good, though...'til she stopped when you weren't expecting it."

His voice carried an undertone of respect, and the small concession made Prudence grateful, although not grateful enough to agree to marry him. At the very next opportunity, she would escape—without the horse.

A creak from behind the curtain woke Arch. He opened his eyes, but didn't recognize the oblong shadows dangling from a beam. *Where...?* His sleepy mind finally caught up. *Dried herbs. The kitchen.* He'd made a pallet out here so Pru could have the bed.

He rolled over, groaning as his muscles protested. He felt stiff as a corpse. That should've given him a clue. It had been a while since he'd slept on a hard dirt floor. The bed would be so much more comfortable even with Pru in it...especially with Pru in it. Once he convinced her to become his wife.

Faint light shone from orange embers glowing among the ashes. The fire hadn't yet gone out, which meant he hadn't been asleep that long. Maybe Prudence had turned over and the ropes creaked. She had slept like a hibernating bear after taking that hard fall a couple days ago.

When he'd seen her fly over Sophie's withers and hit the ground, his stomach had tied itself into knots, and it hadn't got untangled. What a damn fool thing to do, whistling for the horse to stop. He should've realized Pru didn't have a good seat and might pitch off.

None of it would've happened if he'd taken her back to town like she'd asked...repeatedly. His conscience hadn't stopped nagging since he'd picked her up out of the dirt. When she'd stopped resisting, she had fit right into his arms. Even after he'd brought her back inside, he hadn't wanted to let her go.

Heaving a sigh, Arch dropped his forehead onto his crossed arms. He'd plumb lost his mind. Why hang onto a woman who was afraid of him and despised him, not without good reason. He had a mean reputation, mostly on account of his illegal business and his brothers' antics. Nevertheless, Pru would be better off married to him than to whoever might offer for her after she got labeled ruined goods, a bootlegger's leavings. Worse could happen if nobody wed her.

He had selfish reasons, too. Marrying her would be better than dealing with all the trouble her abduction would stir up. His brothers would go to jail. Even if he remained free, no decent woman would come near him after this got around. The railroad sure as hell wouldn't reward him with a clear deed.

Talk about being between a rock and a hard place; he'd set up his pallet there, and could feel every sharp point and unresisting stone.

Shush.

Arch raised his head at the sound. He stared at the wool blanket he'd nailed up to give Pru more privacy. He'd threatened to take the curtain away if she tried to run, and prayed she wouldn't test him.

The blanket rippled.

What the devil was she thinking? He'd taken away his coat and every stitch of clothing except for that nearly transparent shift she wore, which somehow seemed more provocative than if she'd paraded around nude. He'd even hammered a board across the window so she couldn't get out that way. Told her it was for her own good. She'd looked at him like he held the keys to Andersonville Prison.

A shapeless figure appeared from behind the end of the blanket and moved toward the door, inch by slow inch. He could see well enough to make out the quilt wrapped around her. Rebel padded at her heels, his tail waving. He ought to be barking. Worthless muttonhead.

She stopped by the door and bent down, patted the dog's head and offered him something. The smacking sound gave it away. By gum, she'd won over his dog by sneaking treats. Must've hoarded some bread or cheese from the plate of food he'd brought her last night.

Arch's admiration for her ingenuity warred with frustration at her stubbornness. He couldn't stay awake every night watching over her. He couldn't take her back to town, either. She had bruises, stitches in her head, wasn't in any shape to be carted over bumpy roads, even if she had managed to climb on a horse. Not to mention, the soldiers would string him up before he could spit out a good excuse. He'd like to think Pru would stop them, but he wouldn't stake his life on it. He had to convince her to stay put for another week. Buy time to win her over, if that was even possible. If not, he'd get her home safe and then cross the border into Missouri and hide out in the hills until the storm blew over. Then he'd start again with nothing, save his horse.

He pushed up on his elbows. "Don't be foolish, Pru. Go back to bed."

She halted…then put her hand on the latch.

Stubborn woman.

"Unless you want me to carry you to bed—and join you there. I'd prefer sleeping on a feather mattress anyway."

With an aggrieved huff, she spun around and shuffled back the way she came. The blanket quivered. Ropes creaked.

"Your threats won't keep me here..." Her wavering tone told him the threat had worked for the time being.

Arch spent the remainder of the night in fitful sleep. He dragged his stiff body off the floor before dawn and rushed through his chores. He made a mad dash to the creek to fetch water from the spring and milked the cow out in the pasture where he could watch the door. If he didn't get Pru wedded and bedded pretty soon, he'd collapse from pure exhaustion.

Who was the foolish one here? He was going about this the wrong way.

He set the pail of fresh milk on the table, covered it with a cloth to keep out the flies, and then he went to work making flapjacks. She'd won that dog over with treats, and good food always made him happy.

"Treats to sweeten my sour little bride," he said under his breath, chuckling at his clever turn of phrase. He flipped the flat, golden brown discs from the frying pan onto a plate.

Why hadn't he thought of this earlier?

While the coffee pot heated over the hot embers, he went to wake his soon-to-be-wife.

Pru lay curled up on her side, wrapped securely in the quilt, with her hands folded beneath her head. Relaxed in sleep, her features appeared softer. Her skin glowed a warm tone, not pink or gold, but something in between. Loose strands of hair the color of maple syrup lay across her cheek. She looked like the sleeping princess in that poem his ma liked for him to read to her.

Arch smiled as he thought of another way to change her mind about him. Women yearned to be romanced. Leaning down, he hooked his forefinger around the loose hair, stroking her cheek as he drew it back, and whispered in her ear. "Good morning, Sleeping Beauty."

With a gasp, she jerked upwards. The top of her head

struck him on the chin. His teeth snapped together, catching the inside of his lip.

At the sharp pain, he staggered backwards and bumped into the chair, sending it toppling.

She blinked at him with owlish eyes and hugged the quilt to her chin. Her startled confusion turned quickly to irritation. "What are you doing?"

"Wakin' you up." Smiling hurt his lip, but he couldn't help laughing at himself for having such a harebrained idea. "How's your head?"

Frowning, she rubbed the spot that had connected with his chin. "Fine, I think."

"That's good. I fixed us some breakfast. Flapjacks."

Her perturbed expression softened. Her mouth looked much prettier when she didn't have her lips drawn in tight like she'd pulled a drawstring. He would like to taste that pouty lower lip, but surprising her with a kiss would earn him a fist in the face. He had to woo her, carefully, to avoid injury.

"That's very kind of you to prepare breakfast. I'm sorry I won't be able to join you."

His stomach sank. "You don't like flapjacks?"

"Oh no, I love flapjacks. But I can't come to the table wrapped in a quilt."

She could come to the table in her shift as far as he was concerned. Wasn't as if he hadn't seen the parts of her she was so determined to hide. Nice parts, too. Formed to fit into a man's hands... He dragged his attention from her chest to her face.

He hadn't anticipated her refusal. Especially with flapjacks involved. She'd prove harder to win over than Rebel. Good thing he'd come prepared to negotiate.

Pulling a chambray shirt off his shoulder, he tossed it on the bed. "Wear one of my shirts for now. I'll return your things after you eat breakfast with me."

Chapter Four

Delicious smells filled the cabin. Prudence drew back the blanket separating the room and peeked out. Arch squatted by the stone fireplace with his back to her. He appeared to be tending to a coffeepot on an iron spider perched over the coals.

Two places were set at the table. A spray of wild flowers filled a mason jar.

He'd been acting very odd, whispering in her ear and tickling her cheek to wake her, coaxing her with a delicious meal, insisting she wear his shirt… What was he up to?

Taking a deep breath to steady her nerves, she stepped out into the room, curling her toes in the deerskin rug covering the hard-packed dirt. Her stomach urged her onward. She wouldn't give in except for his promise to return her clothes and shoes.

"You said something about flapjacks…"

He twisted around and stood, his eyes widening with surprise, as if he'd forgotten he told her to come to the table wearing only his shirt.

She clutched the front placket. Though the shirttails

reached well past her knees, she felt exposed. Indecent. "Can we please sit down?"

"Of course..." He pulled out a chair, flashing the boyish smile that took her breath away. "I hope you're hungry."

"I'd be hungrier if I was properly dressed."

His gaze dropped lower, past her hips. Oh dear. She shouldn't have said anything to bring his attention to her state of undress.

Tugging the shirttail, she sat down and pulled the chair in as far as she could go, wishing for a tablecloth she could hide under. The sight of a woman's limbs could drive a man into a sexual frenzy. Or so she'd heard. Her mother had been so concerned that she'd made little skirts to cover the lower limbs of the piano.

Arch sat in the chair opposite. He didn't appear to be on the verge of losing control. Evidently, her limbs weren't exciting enough to inspire him. She refused to be disappointed.

The square of unbleached cloth folded up next to the plate looked large enough to cover her chest, all the better. Too bad he hadn't given her the flour sack to wear, instead of cutting it up.

"Let's eat before the food gets cold." Arch poured milk into a mug and set it in front of her before lifting the platter of flapjacks. "Here you go. Take all you want."

Prudence stared at the tall stack. He'd prepared enough to feed the army stationed outside of town. He must be very hungry. She forked two golden brown cakes over to her plate. "They look delicious. Are flapjacks a favorite of yours?"

"Feed me flapjacks an' I'll be happier than a pig wallowing in fresh mud." His disarming grin caught her off guard and she fumbled with her fork.

Arch didn't bat an eye at her flustered response, he

kept holding out the platter piled to the ceiling with flapjacks. An image of pigs sitting in mud, working their way through the enormous stack popped into her head.

She swallowed a laugh. "Thank you, two is enough."

"Have three."

He must think she was one of those pigs. "Gluttony is a sin."

"I'm pretty sure God won't send you to perdition for having three flapjacks." He pulled three onto his plate to prove a point. "See? No lightning bolt."

"Blasphemer," she remarked dryly. "I wouldn't stand under a tree, if I were you."

"Well I'm hungry, so I'm not putting them back. You can say a prayer for me."

She halted with her fork in midair. Why, she'd forgotten to say grace. What was she thinking about? A charming heathen, that's what preoccupied her mind. "Thank you for the reminder."

Prudence bowed her head and prayed aloud, asking God to bless the food, forgive her lapse and to rescue her from heathens. She added a prayer for Arch's soul. After all, he had asked for one.

He added a hearty *Amen*, and dragged two more flapjacks onto his plate, then drenched them in syrup. "Praying makes me hungry."

"And eating makes you happy...like that pig you were talking about."

Laughter burst out of him.

Thank goodness he hadn't taken offense. Sometimes even her family didn't realize when she was joking. Her grandfather had always known. Most folks called him acerbic. He could *carve meat with his tongue*, was what her mother used to say. Prudence had picked up rather early that her grandfather wasn't being serious...most of the time.

"Sis, marry a man with a sense of humor. Not one like your father."

Her grandfather would've liked Arch. She was beginning to like him, too. Not enough to marry him.

She spread butter over her flapjacks and drizzled syrup. "These look good. You do all your own cooking?"

His laughter faded to a wry chuckle. "If I want to eat."

A smile tugged at her lips. She tamed it before it got away from her. Being too friendly would encourage him.

The fork had two tines, an old style like the kind her grandparents had used. Using a tin knife, she cut a small bite and guided it into her mouth, seeing no reason to starve herself while she remained in custody.

He fisted his fork as if he intended to stab the stack of flapjacks and shove the whole thing into his mouth. She paused, holding her fork properly. When he shifted his grip on the utensil, she knew he'd picked up on her silent clue.

"Forget sometimes," he muttered. "Most days, nobody's around to care."

Prudence lowered her gaze. What he'd certainly meant as an offhand remark weighed heavy on her heart. She knew how it felt to be lonely and to wonder whether anyone cared. Why the charming rascal wasn't married by now had to be on account of a shortage of women. He didn't strike her as a man who would be lonely, otherwise.

Arch continued eating. Painstakingly, he cut each bite and lifted it to his mouth. One bite didn't quite make it without syrup dripping down his chin. He caught the sticky drop and licked his finger. The napkin remained folded, by his plate.

She didn't say anything. No need to embarrass him.

He realized his mistake almost immediately. With a

sigh, he wiped off his finger and tucked the flour sack napkin under his chin. The uneven edges looked as if he'd used a knife to cut up the pieces, and he'd sliced right through the black lettering. Odd, when washed, the ink usually faded. This must be the first time he'd used them.

Prudence touched the napkin at her chin. The new napkins, the nice meal, flowers picked for the table, even the sweet way he'd tried to wake her, were the actions of man showing his affection for a woman. She caught a sharp breath. *No.* That couldn't be true. Even when she'd tried, she hadn't been one to inspire men to fawn over her, and she had treated Arch with distrust and disinterest.

All this special attention had to be an act to change her mind about marrying him, although his motives remained unclear. A comment his brother had made niggled at the back of her mind. He'd said Arch needed a wife to secure his land.

The issues were complicated and she didn't understand the technicalities, but she had picked up enough to know that the settlers had arrived first, but the railroad owned the land. The resulting disagreements had erupted into riots, which led to the presence of troops. It wasn't difficult to figure out that the railroad's decision to import women was a kind of bribe to gain the settlers' cooperation. Presumably, Arch needed a wife because the railroad had a policy of giving preferential treatment to married men.

If they wed, he would be able to secure his land and at the same time, protect his brothers.

"Here, have more. I made plenty." He held out the platter, which hardly looked touched.

"Thank you, no. I've had all I want."

Having breakfast with him had been a mistake. She didn't want to be flattered by this younger man's attention, or become closer to him, or feel sympathy or tenderness. She wanted to get her clothes and leave and put this behind her.

"Don't you like it?" he asked.

"Yes, the flapjacks are delicious, but I'm not hungry anymore."

"Does your head hurt?" The concern in his expression and voice put a knot in her throat. She refused to accept his tender ministrations. He'd prevented her from leaving.

"No, I'm feeling much better."

"Don't sound like you're much better."

"I will be much better after you give me my clothes." She laid her fork and knife across the plate. "Please return my things. I've held up my end of the bargain."

He mopped up syrup and popped a large bite into his mouth, chewing slowly and swallowing before he spoke. "Can I trust you not to run?"

"That wasn't part of our deal."

"I won't let you leave on your own, so get that idea outta your head."

"You can give me a ride into town."

He set down his fork, wearing a thoughtful expression. "What'll happen, do you think? After folks find out where you've been and who you've been with. What will people say? How will they look at you?"

Her spotless reputation was the most valuable thing she had to offer. Without it, she couldn't hope to attract the sort of man she wished to marry. Arch knew this and the swine thought to frighten her into cooperating. She lifted her chin and held his eyes with all the defiance she could muster. "I'll tell them the truth."

"You know as well as I do, the truth won't matter."

The truth had to matter. She hadn't stepped over the bounds of propriety. She'd followed the rules, obeyed the teachings her father and mother had drummed into her head from the time she was an infant. She didn't deserve to be punished.

Curse him, he was right, though. Her innocence wouldn't matter. She could scream the truth from the rooftops and people would believe she'd been molested, or worse, had given up her virtue without a fight. Men might dally with ruined women, but they didn't marry them.

His frank gaze turned sympathetic. "You don't have to go back and face all that. I'm offering you marriage."

Wounded and angry, Prudence averted her eyes. He wanted her to think of him as a dashing hero, a prince wielding a gleaming sword, slicing away the barbed briars imprisoning her. The fiend. He watered the bushes and encouraged them to grow by keeping her here. He hadn't wanted to return her from the start.

"My reputation isn't your primary concern. You're worried if I go back I'll cause trouble."

He leaned against the chair back and crossed his arms over his chest, frowning. "That doesn't mean I'm not sincere about wanting to marry you."

Hurt and disappointment carved a hollow place inside her chest. The emptiness was worse than the pain. "You want to marry me for *your* benefit, not mine. At least be honest."

Arch heaved a sigh. He rubbed his hands over his eyes like he was trying to scrub away fatigue. He'd combed his hair and put on a fresh shirt, but that didn't hide the dark circles from lack of sleep. She felt no satisfaction from knowing she was the cause.

He regarded her with a weary expression. "Then let's both be honest. I need a wife. You came out here to get married. If you want a husband, the best way to get one and preserve your reputation is to marry me. It's simple as that."

"Simple? Nothing about this is *simple*." Her future

had been demolished. She couldn't return and pick up where she'd left off, as a respectable woman; and to top it off, she was stuck in the middle of nowhere with a man she couldn't trust.

She threw her napkin on her plate. "I can't accept a proposal from someone who would abduct me and keep me prisoner."

Surprise flashed across Arch's face. Then his expression turned thunderous. "Let's get one thing straight. I didn't know about my brothers' plans and wouldn't have approved if I had. And, you are *not* my prisoner. I've been taking care of you, feeding you, making sure you don't get sick, or run off and get hurt again."

His kindness confused her because it didn't make sense, except as a tool to manipulate her. "Yes, well, I wouldn't think you were in cahoots with your good-for-nothing brothers if you weren't so determined to prevent me from leaving."

"For Pete's sake, Pru..." Arch threw his hands up, making a sound of frustration. "I'm *protecting* you."

"You're protecting yourself and your brothers. I'd be soft in the head if I thought otherwise."

A muscle in his jaw flexed. He clenched his teeth rather than let out whatever he was thinking. Without a word, he jerked back the chair and collected their plates, dumped the uneaten portions into a bucket. The plates clattered as he set them in the sink. Why did he behave as if he were the one offended?

Her hands trembled as she picked up the napkin she'd thrown down in a fit of anger and folded it. Arch unraveled her self-control faster than anyone. She had difficulty thinking straight when she couldn't stop her pulse from racing every time she looked at him. The lingering headache didn't help. That wasn't his fault, though, and she wouldn't complain. He'd been kind, regardless of his motive. She would give him the benefit of doubt and accept that he'd kept her here out of concern. Even so, she wouldn't marry a man solely because she had no choice.

"I'm grateful for what you've done, but I am feeling better and I wish to return to town. I am not your responsibility."

Rather than respond, he crossed over to the fireplace. She was beginning to see a pattern, avoidance versus confrontation. "Will you return my things, as you promised?"

"After we're finished with breakfast." He brought back the coffee pot and poured her a cup, acting like their argument hadn't happened. "You need time to heal. Stay a few more days and rest. Once you get to feeling better, you might change your mind about leaving."

Prudence put a brush Arch had given her to work and then plaited her hair, securing the end with a leather tie. She peered into a mirror above the washstand, gingerly touching the thread holding the skin together along her hairline. A scar was unavoidable. However, it could be worse if Arch hadn't taken care to make fine stitches. The irritating man could be thoughtful, at times.

Thank goodness, he'd returned her clothing.

She smoothed her hands over the rumpled skirt. One sleeve was torn at the elbow and the bodice was stained from dirt and dried blood, which must've happened when she fell and hit her head. If there were other tears or stains, she couldn't see them in the small mirror.

What did it matter? She knew how dowdy she looked, and refused to care. She wasn't trying to impress Arch—other than impressing upon him her desire to leave. Oh, he claimed she wasn't his *prisoner*. But what else should she call it...a well-guarded houseguest?

She peeked around the end of the blanket.

He sat in a chair, pulling on a pair of heavy work boots. She hoped he'd changed his mind about taking her back to town.

"Are we going somewhere?"

"No, *we* aren't. You're staying here and resting while I get some plowing done." He eyed her with a look that said he wasn't going far enough to lose sight of her if she tried to escape.

Running away would be a vain endeavor, as well as foolish. She had no idea how far they were from town, and wandering off on her own in an uncivilized wilderness was paramount to self-murder. She could see that, now that she was less afraid of him. She needed a better plan.

"My head isn't hurting, and I'm feeling much stronger. Thank you for breakfast..."

She spied the pail of milk and a butter churn and an idea came to her. If the way to win a man's heart was through his stomach, it stood to reason he could *lose* interest via the same path.

"Why don't I return the favor and fix the next meal?"

The poor man looked so relieved she almost felt sorry for him. Almost.

"Sounds good to me. You'll get sick of my menu real quick. Flapjacks for breakfast, flapjacks for dinner, flapjacks for supper..." He flashed a self-deprecating smile. "Get the idea?"

"Oh, yes..." She certainly did. Like all men, he wanted a wife who could cook. Once he tasted her *cooking*, he wouldn't be able to get rid of her fast enough.

He tucked the worn denims into the top of his boots. "That field needs to be plowed to prepare it for corn. I'm already behind schedule. Good thing I got Sophie. Otherwise, I'd need a team of oxen to pull a plow blade through that thick grass."

"I can imagine... I've never seen such a large, powerful horse."

Standing, he adjusted his suspenders, which looked to be made from old mattress ticking. His wide shoulders and muscled arms pulled at the shirt, which had faded to a light blue that matched his eyes. His rough clothing enhanced rather than detracted from his appeal.

Prudence tried—but failed—to look away. Appreciating how well God had made him was no sin. Except, she had to stop appreciating him and get busy ruining his next meal.

Instead of leaving, Arch followed her to the fireplace. "Sophie is strong as an ox and loads smarter. I bought her from a fellow that brought heavy draft horses over from France. Plan to have my own herd one day. Drafts like Sophie can haul heavy loads—like railroad ties— easy as pie. Strong horses will be in high demand with all the railroad and mining construction..."

Sounded like he had a dream and plan. She respected a man with initiative. However, the man she married wouldn't start a courtship by holding her against her will.

Prudence sorted through cookware scattered around the fireplace. She needed something to use to heat milk. Not a frying pan. This long-handled pot would do. "Have you considered putting nails in the hearth and hanging your pots and utensils? It would be easier to find the right ones, and they wouldn't get as dirty."

"Good idea." Arch leaned in from behind and his breath stirred a curl by her ear. "I'll be back in time for dinner. Don't miss me too much."

His hand came in contact with her backside in a fond pat.

Shocked, she whirled around, intending to slap him.

He leapt out of the way, and the aggravating rogue started laughing. "Don't brain me with that pot! You'll be stitching up *my* head!"

"Then cease your familiarities." She backed up to a work surface next to the sink, which was nothing more than two boards set atop barrels. Snatching up a cloth, which appeared to be clean, she wiped dust out of the pot. Her hands shook. All he'd done was pat her through layers of clothing. Inappropriate, yes, and startling. But her body hummed at his touch like a metal rod struck by lightning. She hadn't experienced this strange reaction to any other man's touch. Not even men she had liked.

With effort, she focused her attention on pouring milk into the pot and then set it to warm on the same iron spider he'd used to heat the coffee.

Arch put on a wide-brimmed hat made from woven straw. Pausing at the door, he watched her. Rather than leaving, he returned to peer over her shoulder. "What are you doing?

She maintained an air of nonchalance despite being nervous at his suspicion. "If you heat the milk a little, it will make the cream rise more quickly. I'll be able to churn it into butter faster."

His forehead furrowed as he absorbed her explanation. She held her breath, praying he knew less about making butter than making flapjacks. "Don't recall Ma mentioning anything like that, but if it cuts down on your work, have at it."

He stopped on his way out and took down a rifle mounted over the door. Her father had taken a pistol to the fields in case of snakes. In all that grass, there had to be more than a few reptiles. That was something to keep in mind.

After he exited, whistling, she sighed with relief.

She moved the pot closer to the hot coals. Heating

milk a little did help the cream rise. Scalding the milk would guarantee the butter would be ruined.

Her stomach knotted. Never had she purposely wasted food, and to do so seemed a sin. But making him want to be rid of her would be preferable to running away, or giving in to this irrational attraction. He sensed her weakness and would exploit it if she weren't careful.

"Don't follow the desires of your sinful nature…"

She would do well to heed her father's admonition this time.

Arch needed a wife rather like he needed that horse. As for her, she didn't expect a love match, but she refused to settle for convenience. She might be willing to marry a stranger, but it would be one she picked out, not one that was forced on her.

Several hours later, she'd finished the butter, baked two loaves of bread and put beans on to cook in a Dutch oven. Perspiring from the heat, she went out in search of a breeze.

In a field where the tall grass had been cut down, Arch struggled behind a plow. His mare looked to be working hard, too. Man and beast strained together. The both of them extraordinary, beautiful creatures, and well suited to settling this land.

She had hoped to marry a hardworking farmer and live on land that would grow about anything. Arch had fenced a pasture and put up stables for the animals. He had a good cow that produced rich milk and pigs growing fat in a pen. The chickens ranged free and roosted in the tall grass right alongside the prairie hens. A henhouse would provide better protection. If she were living here, she would insist he build one. But she wouldn't be living here, so what he did with his chickens was his own business.

Arch moved out of sight, the house blocking her

view. Just as well. She had to stop watching him and pining for him. Had he come courting, she would've been pleased by his interest, and if convinced of his integrity and respect, she would have considered him. But he hadn't come to see her, even though he'd stated he needed a wife and she was one of the few marriageable women in town. He wouldn't have selected her if he'd had a choice, either.

Banishing the sobering thought, she mopped her damp forehead with a napkin. The air was cooler out here, but she felt hot, and dirty and desperate for a bath. She'd seen no tub, but she could put down an oilcloth and make do with a bucket of clean water.

The farm abutted a wooded area with a spring-fed creek that wasn't too far away.

She closed the clapboard door hung on leather hinges and lowered a piece of wood to lock it shut. That wouldn't keep out humans, but it would prevent animals from getting inside.

"Rebel, here boy!" she called to the dog. Arch's hound would alert her to snakes or other dangerous creatures.

As Prudence strolled across the clearing, Rebel zigzagged in front her with his nose to the ground. He got along on three legs fine, and didn't resent his infirmity or complain about his lot in life. In fact, he looked like he was always smiling.

In a sense, the dog reminded her of Arch. Of course, Arch wasn't missing limbs. His were all intact and nicely formed, and she spent far too much time thinking about them. He and Rebel were alike in that they both had a sunny outlook and disposition...and neither of them would let her wander off alone.

At the edge of the woods, three dark-skinned, bare-chested men stepped out from the trees.

Her heart lodged in her throat. *Indians.*

They came to a halt at the same time she did. If they were surprised to see her, she couldn't tell. Their faces might've been carved from walnut, being so devoid of movement or expression.

Rather than war paint and feathers, the Indians wore an odd assortment of clothing: a patched frock coat without a shirt, a bow tie around a bare neck, feathers stuck into the band of a battered top hat. Two men sported breechcloths and moccasins. The third had fringed leggings paired with a red silk vest. Shiny black braids hung over their shoulders.

Rebel bounded up from wherever he'd been and stood, fur bristling, between her and the three men. A low growl rumbled up from the hound's chest.

The Indian in the top hat raised an old flintlock rifle.

"No!" She rushed to kneel beside Rebel and wrapped her arm around his loose-skinned neck, petting him to let him know she was all right. God forbid they would kill him simply for protecting her.

The other Indians, who appeared to be younger, were armed with bows slung across their backs. They didn't reach for their arrows. If they did, she didn't have a gun.

She glanced over her shoulder. Arch was nowhere in sight. If Rebel barked, he would come running. But then the Indian might shoot him. Or they might kill her and scalp her before he could cross the distance between them.

Prudence fought the panic rising in her throat. Somehow, she had to communicate to these men, convince them she meant them no harm. "The dog won't hurt you, if you don't hurt me."

The man wearing the feathered top hat lowered his gun. "Want food."

Top Hat spoke English, or a smattering. If she could make herself understood, she might be able to convince them to leave. She couldn't serve these Indians the special meal she'd prepared for Arch. They would kill her, thinking she was trying to poison them.

"I'm sorry. No food."

The Indian's black brows slashed in a fierce frown that sent a chill down her spine. She had read about Indian attacks where women had been taken captive and degraded.

Her body quaked, an uncontrollable reaction to terror.

The dog's growls grew louder. If she withered beneath her fear, Rebel might attack and things would go badly for both of them. From what she'd read, Indians respected courage. Even if she didn't have any, she could pretend.

She patted the dog and then stood, shoulders squared. "All right, I'll get you food, but I'm giving you no guarantee you'll like it."

Top Hat kept the gun trained on the dog. He lifted his chin, indicating she should go toward the house. What choice did she have?

As she drew near the cabin, she prayed Arch would see her even though she couldn't see him. Of course, the annoying man wasn't in sight when she needed him.

Rebel stayed close, every so often growling to let the Indians know he was watching them.

When she reached the door she instructed the three men to wait outside. They didn't wait. They followed her into the house.

Now what?

Rebel slipped inside, remaining close, as if he sensed that she needed him. The dog couldn't protect her against three armed men, but she felt better with him in the house. If bad went to worse, he would sound an alarm, and maybe Arch would arrive before the Indians murdered them both.

The bronze-skinned savage with the red silk vest went to the table and lifted the cloth off the bread. He picked up a loaf and held it in the air like a prize. The one wearing the bow tie around his neck started poking around the fireplace. He motioned for her to get the Dutch oven.

She had no choice. The Indians had made it clear they wanted food and she had better give it to them. After one bite, they wouldn't be coming back for more.

Top Hat cradled the rifle, watching as she set the beans on the table with what she'd swear was amusement in his dark eyes. Would they take the food and leave? She prayed that would be the case. If they tasted it before they left, they might decide to take her scalp along as well.

"Here, let me spoon some in a bowl. You can take it with you…"

The Indian wearing the bow tie swiped the ladle out of her hand. He dipped into the pot and brought the hot beans to his lips, blew across them, and then took a big bite.

Prudence held her breath. The beans had to taste atrocious. She'd burned the bottom, undercooked them, and to make sure, stirred in some lye soap.

The Indian's face remained set, impassive, except for the moisture welling in his eyes. Without a word, he handed the ladle to the man in the red silk vest.

He took a bite; his expression also remained flat, save for the flaring of his nostrils. Inexplicably, the second man dipped the spoon into the beans, and then offered it to the third, the older man.

Top Hap took the ladle. He didn't spare the other two a glance and began to eat. After the first bite, he stopped. The glimmer of amusement in his black eyes fled, replaced by flat disdain. He picked up a loaf, turned it in his hands and then banged it on the table.

The younger Indian who held the second loaf watched him with wide eyes, and then set the second brick-hard loaf back where he'd found it.

A shuffling noise came from the doorway. Rebel whined, but didn't bark.

Arch entered the house with a rifle in his hands.

Prudence sagged with relief. Thank God, he hadn't stumbled in unawares. Though it had taken him long enough to get here. If she'd hightailed it, he would've been on her trail before she reached the end of his property.

"What's goin' on here?" He asked the question in a casual tone, as if inquiring about the weather. His gun wasn't pointed at the threat. He had it aimed at the floor. Of course, the Indians didn't appear a bit frightened. They seemed so sure he wouldn't shoot them that none of them went for their weapons. They regarded him with the same inscrutable expressions they'd worn since recovering from their surprise upon meeting her at the creek.

"You said we could come hunt. We smelled food. Got hungry."

Prudence gaped at the man in the top hat. So, he knew more English than he'd let on, and it seemed he knew Arch, too. He hadn't mentioned that, although she doubted the knowledge would've made her more inclined to let them in.

Top Hat said something to one of the younger men, a guttural phrase, and gestured to the door. The man in the red silk vest and the one in the bow tie walked past Arch without speaking. He didn't stop them. But he did act surprised by their abrupt departure.

She wasn't surprised. They'd lost their appetite.

The older Indian dropped the bread loaf on the table. It landed with a heavy thud. He gave her a disapproving frown and then exited behind the other two men. On his way out, he spoke to Arch. "You need a new wife. That one's no good."

Prudence didn't utter a sound after the Indian departed. Her face had gone as pale as a bleached bone. Poor thing. She had to be scared out of her wits.

Arch propped the rifle near the door, went over to her and took her into his arms without a word. She didn't push him away. Instead, she grabbed ahold of his shirt and clung to him, trembling. He held her close and gently rubbed her back.

"It's all right," he crooned against her hair, even though nothing was *all right* about finding her in the house alone with three Indians. Fortunate for her, these men were trustworthy and honorable, but they could've been Kiowa raiders or no-account white men, both equally dangerous.

"You're safe now," he murmured.

She turned her face into his shoulder. "No…you're wrong. I'll never be safe here."

Her woeful statement pricked his conscience. Little wonder she felt that way. Despite his denial, he had kept her a virtual prisoner. Then he'd gone off and left her without protection. He'd been so intent on the backbreaking work, he hadn't seen anyone come up to the house. Something had told him to go check on her and he'd grabbed his rifle. Hadn't needed it, but he didn't know that before he came in the door.

"Those Indians were no danger to you. The older one in the top hat is *Mahzee*. He's a Potawatomi chief, and those are his sons. Their territory is south of here. I've told the chief he can hunt on my land. Sometimes we share a meal."

Arch curled his hand around Pru's neck. The hair growing there was even softer and silkier. He longed to put his lips where his fingers were at the moment, but he'd better not. She wasn't in an amorous mood, even if she seemed comfortable in his arms. For now, she was willing to let him massage her neck, an improvement over conking him with a pot.

She slid her hands up to his chest as if to make sure he was really there. Maybe she was so stunned she didn't realize she was touching him. "I've never seen an Indian before."

"Never? Where did you live?"

"Ohio."

"They don't have Indians in Ohio?"

"Not anymore."

Wanting to soothe her, he began to rub the tense muscles on the back of her shoulders. She responded by moving her hands to his arms and squeezing. His muscles flexed, an instinctive reaction. Not so instinctive, the quivering excitement racing through him and the dizzying sensation of being swept into an irresistible current.

He took a deep breath. She didn't intend to arouse him. At most, she touched him like she was exploring unfamiliar terrain. That didn't change the fact that he couldn't control his body's reaction. He could, however, control his behavior.

"I feared you wouldn't come back in time." She rested her head against his shoulder. Now *that* was a surprise. Maybe this incident hadn't been such a bad thing after all. She seemed to be warming up to him. He was getting warmer, for sure. "I didn't even have a gun."

He trailed his fingertip along the edge of her ear, encouraged when she shivered but didn't pull away. "If I'd left you a gun, you might've shot the chief, or one of his sons. Then we'd have real trouble on our hands."

"You won't give me the means to protect myself?" She looked up at him, her dark eyes anxious. He longed to see them shine with trust, and grow warm with desire.

"'Course I will. So long as you know who it is you ought to be shooting."

"I'll start with you."

Her biting humor had returned. She must be feeling better.

"How do you know those Indians?" she asked.

"I lived near them when I was growing up. There's lots of Indians out here, most of them friendly, the ones that live in the Territory, that is. Like us, they want a place to call their own and to raise their families in peace. Trouble starts when men get greedy."

"Those Indians didn't seem friendly."

"Oh, that was them being real friendly. I'm surprised they didn't stay to eat."

She averted her eyes, as if something he said embarrassed her. "The chief doesn't think I'd be a good wife…"

Arch tipped her chin so she would look at him again. "It isn't the chief who wants to marry you."

Her lips parted, a look of surprise, or it could be alarm. Rather than hear her voice another rejection, he bent his head and covered her mouth. Talking never got them anywhere. Kissing might. He'd enjoy it, regardless.

The moment his mouth touched hers, she sewed her lips shut. He would've taken it to mean she didn't want the kiss, but the way she kept squeezing his arms said she did. Maybe she didn't know how because she was inexperienced. That would explain why she got so jumpy whenever he got close. She came to him innocent. He'd never gotten such a precious gift. In return, he would show her, and teach her, what he knew about giving. Granted, his sexual experience wasn't vast, but he'd learned enough to know how to bring a woman pleasure.

First, he had to teach Pru how to kiss.

He brushed light kisses over her tight lips, teased the seam with his tongue. When she didn't release the pucker, he whispered against her mouth. "Relax your lips, let me show you…"

Her lips opened like the petals of a shy flower. He slanted his mouth across hers and demonstrated how men and women went about kissing.

Initiating his bride-to-be gave him a heady rush. Her eagerness took his breath away. She wasn't the only one learning how good a kiss could be.

Her hands crept upward. She stroked his shoulders, explored the dip above his collarbone, and then wrapped her arms around his neck and leaned closer, pressing her soft breasts against his chest.

Desire roared through him with the force of a spring twister.

He tightened his hold around her waist. *Patience.* No matter how hot she made him burn, he couldn't rush this, or he'd spoil the moment and not get another chance. Despite her fervent response, she was skittish as a yearling and distrustful. He had to show her, not tell her, that she could trust him.

With every kiss, she seemed to gain confidence. Her ardor tested his self-control. He longed to devour her; to strip her bare and put his mouth on her skin, bring her to readiness, as she'd done to him. As their tongues met and danced, he ran his hands down her back, cupped her buttocks and drew her full against him.

He couldn't restrain a moan.

At the sound, she stiffened. Then she broke away, pushing at his chest, and backed out of his arms with a gasp. Or was that a sob? He couldn't tell because she'd spun around.

She grabbed a wooden spoon from the table and turned, raising it like a club. Some women liked to get a little rough. Generally they didn't use a wooden spoon, or look bug-eyed with fear.

Pru wasn't playing. She'd retreated and put up a defense—a wooden spoon. She could construct a stone fortress and it wouldn't keep him out.

"Don't touch me." Her sultry tone didn't match her command. Neither did the high color in her face or her heaving chest. She'd been as affected as him by that kiss. He could advance. Win the battle. If he did, he would lose the war. He had to let her walk away, as many times as she needed. Only with patience could he bring her to him.

He opened his palms in the universal gesture for surrender. "I won't touch you if you don't want me to…give you my word."

She backed away another step, casting her eyes from side to side, as if looking for a way out. Rebel came off the ratty blanket near the fireplace and stretched. He sniffed at her skirts. She reached down and drew the dog closer. His hound would provide no protection from the things she feared. Even Rebel seemed to know this, and rubbed his head against her skirts.

"He's telling you not to be afraid."

Pru glared. "What does the dog know? You didn't accost him."

Another defense, that prim, prickly exterior. Pru hid her passionate nature well—until she'd kissed him. Arch resisted the urge to smile. "I didn't accost you, either. I kissed you, and you kissed me back." He wet his lips. "Very nicely, I might add."

Her cheeks flushed, which would've been pretty had she not narrowed her eyes. "I won't let you lure me into sin."

She'd been attending too many tent meetings.

"That didn't feel like sin to me, was too good to be bad."

"Sacrilegious heathen."

This time he did smile. She ruffled up her feathers like a prairie hen trying to scare away a predator. "How come you're so scared when you know I won't hurt you? I'd love you real good...if you'd let me."

Shock flashed across of her face, followed by stark fear. "Love! You aren't offering me love. Don't insult me by trying to disguise your intentions. You want to...to..." She jabbed the spoon at him, finishing her thought with what she might not have realized was a crude gesture. "Because you think I'm a foolish old maid you can trick into falling for your advances, so I won't report you or your conniving brothers."

Arch dropped his arms. Her accusation wasn't exactly true, but close enough to make him feel guilty about marrying her to suit his own interests. She seemed to think it was impossible for him to have any genuine feelings for her. Either she considered him incapable of tender emotions or she feared she couldn't inspire them.

Facing off made her more defensive, so he took a seat at the table and picked up a bread loaf. The thing felt heavy as a sod brick. He tried to break it in half. Finally, he took his penknife to pry off a piece. Maybe she'd gotten distracted and left the pan in the coals too long. "Why do you doubt that I could desire you, or have a care for you?" he asked in a non-threatening tone.

She pushed the second loaf out of his reach, for some odd reason, and stepped back, as if she feared he might make a grab for her. "What a foolish question. You're a healthy young man. Look at me. I'm plain and thirty and have never been married. I'm a dried-up old maid."

Arch gave her curvy form a good look-over like she'd asked. "You don't look dried up to me."

Her cheeks flushed the color of a ripe peach.

"And you're pretty when you blush."

This bread, on the other hand, was dry as winter wood. Maybe butter would soften it. He dipped his knife into a small crock filled with whitish yellow butter that had flakes in it. He couldn't remember butter ever looking flaky.

She eyed the buttered bread with frowning concern. Apparently, she was aware that the butter wasn't quite right. He didn't want to complain and make her feel even worse about herself.

"You don't have to say things you know aren't true."

Her accusation annoyed him. His motives might be suspect, but not his honor.

"You think I'm lying?" If kissing hadn't convinced her that he found her desirable, saying it wouldn't make her believe him, but he had to try to get through to her so she would stop finding excuses to refuse him. "Surely somebody besides me has told you that you're pretty."

A sad, wistful look came into her eyes. "A long time ago…"

"Did he ask for your hand?"

Instead of answering, she reached for the bowls she'd put on the table. He took one before she could whisk them away. "I've received several proposals. None were from the kind of man I'd marry."

"Ah, so you're picky…"

"No, I have standards."

"Having standards isn't a bad thing. As long as you aren't impossible to please." He bit into the buttered bread—and about broke off his front teeth. He'd offend her if he threw it into the fire. Maybe he could soften it. From the Dutch oven, he dipped out a serving of soupy beans.

"What are your standards for a husband?" He wondered if he met any of them.

"Hard-working. Honest."

He met those two. Mostly.

She put the other bowls into the cupboard, and then came after the beans. Before she took away the pot, he dipped out another spoonful. She ought to know he'd be starved after working all morning. Maybe she was worried about rations.

"And temperate," she added, setting the Dutch oven on the hearth. "That's a must. I stay away from men who indulge in strong drink."

The rock that hit the bottom of Arch's stomach wasn't made from bread. It was a fair bet she would stay *far* away from a man who made his living from selling moonshine.

How long could he hide the truth from her?

Not long enough.

He dipped a piece of bread into his bowl to sop up the liquid, as he mulled over how to present his family's business in a good light. "Whiskey isn't bad…"

"It is when a man loves it so much he ignores his responsibilities and abandons his…the people who depend on him."

Arch stopped with the bread halfway to his mouth. Her halting correction made it clear she wasn't talking in general terms. "Who did that to you?"

"Someone who doesn't matter anymore." She stepped back from the table. The way she kept wringing her hands and glancing at the door made him wonder if she planned to sprint away.

"Why are you so nervous? I'll won't bite, I promise. Now tell me about the fellow that don't matter anymore."

She stopped twisting her fingers and held still. He tried to read her expression: pain, confusion, maybe regret. "We were to be married. At our wedding, after I'd waited for over an hour for him to show up, I found him drunk and passed out in the barn. He tried to apologize and explain, but… Looking back, I should've seen it coming. He carried a flask with him at all times. I consider myself lucky to have escaped."

"You're right. You were lucky." Arch longed to pound whoever had hurt her into the dirt.

"He sounds like a weak man, not someone worthy of you."

"If I'd listened to my father, I might've avoided humiliation. He warned against the ills of liquor and how it can lead to disgrace and dishonor."

Sounded like her strait-laced pa had put the fear of God into her when it came to sex and drinking, two things most men enjoyed.

"That fellow was a bad apple, I'll give you that. But not everyone who drinks turns into a debased drunkard," Arch retorted.

Her pointed look said otherwise. Trying to convince her he wasn't the devil incarnate would take some doing.

He put the soggy bread into his mouth.

Ugh. Tasted awful. Without letting on, he set it on the edge of the plate and tried a spoonful of beans. His throat closed up. Oh God. Worse. He forced down what was in his mouth, rather than spitting it onto the plate.

Pru set a cup in front of him. "Here, have some water."

He downed the cool liquid in three gulps. That helped, though it didn't completely wash away the horrid taste.

She rubbed her hands together anxiously. "You don't like it?"

"It…" He had to be honest because she knew something was wrong and if he fibbed about this, she would assume he'd lie about more important things. "Tastes bitter."

Her cheeks reddened. "I did wash the beans with

69

soap before I cooked them. Maybe I didn't rinse them well enough."

Astonished, he set down the spoon. "You used soap?"

She nodded.

"No wonder it tastes so vile." He rubbed his forehead, as his fond dreams about delicious meals flew out the window. His future wife couldn't make bread and she didn't know the most basic thing about cooking beans. God bless her for trying. "You don't use soap to clean beans. Rinse them in water."

"Oh." She cast a sad look at his plate, went from rubbing her hands to wringing them and looking so distressed that he felt bad for being honest. "I-I'm sure you must think I'm worthless."

Chapter Five

"Worthless?" Arch exclaimed "Because of beans?"

Prudence reached for his bowl and pulled the foul slop away. This time he didn't try to stop her. He'd worked hard all morning and had to be starving and she had denied him sustenance. He'd been kind, protective. She'd deliberately set out to give him a stomachache.

She couldn't deny the passion and attraction that sparked between them, even if she didn't know what to make of it. On the other hand, he ought to be more than ready to get rid of her, so she shouldn't be eaten up with regret.

He stood and came around the table, frowning so fiercely she wondered if he might strike her. She resisted cringing and looked him in the eye.

"I'm sorry, Arch. You deserve better."

He grasped her arm and dragged her to him, astonishingly, embraced her. "Aw, Pru, how do you reckon a spoilt meal makes you worthless? There's nothing further from the truth. The worthless cur is that man who made you doubt yourself."

Stunned, then lightheaded with relief, she clung to him. The only men who'd ever stood up for her were those in her immediate family. Even then, her father and brother had let her believe she was lacking in some way.

She turned her face into Arch's shoulder, breathing in his scent, primitive and purely male. Her hold on him tightened and excitement ignited the now-familiar warmth. "You aren't angry with me?"

"Heck no..." He caressed the back of her head, fondling the length of her plaited hair, his touch possessive, yet at the same time, gentle.

Something inside her chest shifted. Her heart felt lighter. Softer.

He cupped her cheek in a calloused palm. Warm, slightly rough, his touch sent her pulse fluttering at the base of her throat, beneath her wrists and behind her knees. As he bent his head, her legs grew as weak as her willpower.

"I'm not hungry for beans, anyhow," he murmured, an instant before his mouth covered hers. He proved his point by feasting on her lips.

How amazing. She'd rebuffed him at every turn, even laced his food with lye soap, and still he wanted her.

An emotional thunderstorm gathered force. The power of desire ripped away propriety as a strong wind might tear the roof from a house. Heart pounding, she grasped at the hard muscles on his broad back.

With his hands, he shaped her ribcage and waist and then moved downward over her hips. He deepened the kiss, putting his tongue in her mouth as he had before. She welcomed the intimate invasion and even slanted her head to provide a better angle. Desire fueled boldness. She brought her hands around to his chest to explore the hard muscles beneath the soft shirt.

He responded with a rumbling sound, somewhere between a purr and a growl, and drew her up against him, so close she could feel the changes in his body wrought by passion.

The warm flickers of desire flared into a blaze, its flames heating her from the inside out. She longed to throw off her clothes and drag him into bed. An audacious thought, but not the first time she'd entertained the illicit impulse.

Flee from temptation.

Passion's roaring winds nearly drowned out the small voice. Her soul would be in peril should she ignore the warning. Somehow, she found the strength to end the kiss.

Arch gazed down at her with stark hunger darkening his eyes. His features looked sharper and his skin, flushed. His face and body revealed the effects of strong passions. Passions she had inspired. If she had a smidgen of decency, she would be offended. Instead, she exulted in her newly discovered feminine power.

Nevertheless, she hadn't completely lost her mind or her fragile hold on self-respect.

"R-release me," she stammered.

The moment he relaxed his grip, she took a step backwards, needing to get away so she wouldn't give in to the urge to reach for him again. Women who were seduced and led astray became enslaved to sinful cravings. *Fallen angels*, her father had called them. They usually ended up in brothels.

"You promised you wouldn't touch me." She had to hold him to his word because she didn't have the strength to resist.

Regret flickered across his face. "I promised I wouldn't if you don't want me to…"

His reminder of her moral failure brought on a hot blush.

"Don't be scared of what you're feeling, Pru. It's natural."

"All the sins of the flesh are *natural*, but that doesn't make them right." Kissing him had awakened something wanton inside her. She hadn't resisted, hadn't even wanted to resist. "I'm not blaming you. I'm the one who transgressed."

"Transgressed?" He blinked as if the meaning was lost on him. He must not have been raised in a devout household, or he would know what that word meant.

"Women are called to be examples of purity and restraint," she explained. "Men are supposed to flee from ungodliness, too. But being men, they can be forgiven for their animal passions."

"Animal passions?" Arch shook his head with a dry laugh. "You don't know much about animals if you think that was... Ah, never mind. Enjoying a kiss doesn't mean you're impure and unrestrained."

She had kissed him with abandon and had her hands all over him... Why, it made her tremble to think about how truly unrestrained she could be.

"A virtuous woman doesn't *enjoy* kissing." She turned away, blinking back tears of frustration. "It must be my rebellious nature. I've always been too spontaneous and given to...to strong passions."

Nine years ago, her father had caught her in the barn with her sweetheart the night before he marched off to join his company. They hadn't done more than share a few innocent hugs and a quick kiss. But since she had wondered if Will's death was punishment for wanting more. She had vowed never to have immoral thoughts again. Yet, she couldn't seem to control the urges.

"There must be something wrong with me," she bemoaned.

"Hush, now, there's not a thing wrong with you...and I don't reckon God will get mad about a few kisses."

Arch's hands came to rest on her shoulders. She trembled. Heaven forbid he put his arms around her. "If we was to get married, you wouldn't have to worry so much about your virtue."

"You're incorrigible." Prudence tore away from his grasp and fled out the open door.

Arch wasn't certain what *incorrigible* meant, but he knew it wasn't a compliment. He'd kissed her to show her that he valued her and wanted her, so she would feel better about herself. All he'd accomplished was to make her feel worse.

He followed her outside. Might be she'd run for fear he would give in to his *animal passions* again. So, she thought of him as a rutting stallion? Granted, laughing hadn't been the best response, even if her remark had been funny, and sort of a compliment, too, though she hadn't meant it to be.

"Pru, wait, you don't have to run. I won't kiss you—" No, he couldn't make a promise he was sure to break. "Without asking permission."

She swung around, holding onto the rope handle of an empty bucket. "I won't give my permission."

"Then you got nothin' to worry about." He remained a few feet away in case she decided to use the bucket as a weapon. "What do you intend to do with that?"

"I need water…" She looked away like she was embarrassed. "To bathe."

Why on earth would admitting to wanting a bath be shameful? Then again, she'd been taught that anything remotely pleasurable was a sin.

"You can't bathe in a bucket. Wash off in the creek."

She looked at him like he'd lost his mind.

"Absolutely not. I'm not bathing in the creek. What if your Indian friends are out there?"

"I'll stand watch…with my back turned. I swear."

"No, thank you. The scriptures tell us to flee from the Devil." Squaring her shoulders, she started off in the direction of the trees, swinging the bucket by her side.

First, an animal, now the Devil… He wasn't making progress in the right direction.

He caught up with her and grabbed the rope handle. "I've got a tub around here somewhere. Let me get it."

She hesitated to release the bucket, but the longing in her eyes told him he'd already won this argument. "Well, I suppose I could wait until you find the tub. I'll fix us something to eat."

His stomach did a slow flip. He wasn't eager to sample another one of her attempts even if he appreciated the effort. "Don't worry about cooking. There's cheese in the pantry and a tin of sardines and soda crackers. You can pick lettuce and carrots and whatever else you find in the garden that looks ripe."

While she stayed busy, Arch cleaned out a metal tub he'd used in the stables and rolled it over next to the house. After five trips down to the creek with two buckets, he finally filled it deep enough for a bath. On the last trip, he dumped a bucketful of water into a large pot, hung it over the fire pit outside and got a blaze going. While the water heated, he darted into the house and collected sheets off the bed. When she asked what he was doing, he told her to be patient.

He'd landed on a way to improve her mood and show her he wasn't so *incorrigible*.

Using branches and rope, he created a frame for a screen around the tub so she would have privacy. As he draped the sheets over the branches, Rebel sniffed the fabric. The dog might think they were playing a game.

"Leave it alone," he warned. "Unless you want her to lay into you about your *animal passions*."

After he'd poured in the hot water, he invited Pru outside.

"Your bath is ready, Miss Walker." He bowed and gestured, showing her he knew something of fine manners.

Her astonished expression changed to delight when she drew back a sheet and dipped her fingers in the water. "Oh, it's warm! Arch, thank you!" She whirled around, gave him a quick hug, and then vanished behind the sheet. "This is wonderful. You really shouldn't have gone to so much trouble…"

"No trouble." He rolled his aching shoulders. A bath was a simple enough thing, and the effort was worth it to see her so happy. Next time, she might even give him a kiss. After they were married, she could enjoy it, guilt-free.

The sheet rippled. "I'm not sure where to…"

"Hand over your clothes."

The rustling stopped. She was thinking about it. He wagered that her desire for a bath would win out over her obsessive modesty. After another moment, the sheet moved and she thrust out her dress, followed by petticoats, stockings, and a variety of undergarments. "Please put them inside until I'm finished."

After laying out her clothing on the bed, he helped himself to some of the food she'd put out. He could go hunting later. Prairie hens were plentiful, and he could teach Pru how to prepare the birds and roast them. He could teach her other things, as well—pleasure being at the top of the list. Once they were married, she might be more willing to learn. She would take to passion as natural as a duckling went to water.

By now, she ought to be enjoying her bath and feeling more charitable.

He dragged a chair outside and sat down.

Rebel stretched out and put his chin on his paws.

The sound of humming came from behind the sheet. Splashing. More humming.

"You enjoying that bath?"

A gasp was followed by a loud splash. "Arch? I didn't know you were out there."

"Told you I'd keep watch. Rebel might decide to play tug with the sheet."

"Oh dear..." The splashing stopped. He really shouldn't tease her while she was sitting naked in a bathtub.

"Enjoy your bath, Pru. Nobody will bother you, me included. You have my word."

After a moment, she went back to splashing, indicating she both believed him and trusted him enough to be comfortable in a vulnerable situation, another step in the right direction.

Arch drummed his fingers on his knees. He glanced at the sheet. When she'd been sick and feverish, he'd bathed her down. The thin shift hadn't hidden much. He'd glimpsed pink-tipped breasts, the shadow at the juncture of her legs. She had the most tempting body, yet he hadn't taken advantage of her by gawking...more than necessary.

He wasn't an animal and he could control himself.

The sounds she made as she bathed stirred tantalizing images. If he didn't find some distraction, pretty soon he'd soon be in a state that wouldn't be good for either of them—at the present moment.

He started whistling.

"Please, no," she cried. "Don't you know anything besides *Dixie?*"

She'd told him she was from Ohio...a Yankee girl.

"Bonnie Blue Flag?" He stretched out his legs and grinned, waiting.

She rewarded him with a groan. "I should've known

you'd memorize Confederate tunes. You named your dog Rebel."

Arch debated how much to tell her about his past association with a lost cause. No point in denying it. Then again, there was no need to hash it over, either, and get sidetracked on a pointless argument about which side was right. "My brother named him. I took him in after he tangled with a bear."

"Your brother didn't want an injured animal, I take it?"

Obe would've shot the dog.

"He didn't see much use for a hound that can't earn its way."

"How fortunate for Rebel that you and your brother don't agree."

The hound lifted his head at his name. When Arch reached down, Rebel licked his fingers. Most men would've put the animal out of its misery, rather than spending weeks nursing the dog's grievous injuries. He'd known he was being foolishly sentimental, hadn't regretted it, though. He refused to regret his decision to hold onto Pru. She wasn't a three-legged dog, but she needed him...even if she didn't realize it yet.

"Guess I'm soft-hearted," he admitted.

"That's not a flaw."

"Never said it was, but being seen as soft can be dangerous. That's why I don't let too many folks in on my secret."

"I'll keep your secret safe..." Water sloshed. "Would you bring me my clothes?"

"Sure will." He headed inside, smiling and more confident than ever. One bath, and Pru had already softened toward him. A few more favors, and he would gain her agreement to be his wife, and everything would work out fine.

At some point, he had to break the news about the family business. She might not like the idea of being called a bootlegger's wife, but it was more respectable than the alternative.

Chapter Six

Prudence finished dressing behind the screen then drifted inside the house to look for a brush so she could work out the damp tangles. She went behind the curtain and searched around the washstand and on the bed. "Do you know where the brush went?" she called.

"Out here."

Arch stood at the table where he'd pulled out a chair. He held up the boar-bristle brush and smiled suggestively. Unbelievable. He'd already pampered her by preparing a warm bath. Now he wished to perform another service.

"You...you want to brush my hair?" Why, the very idea of allowing the intimacy made her insides quiver. She couldn't call it fear, more like anticipation.

Before she could talk herself out of it, she went to the chair and sat down. A faint, strident voice exhorted, the privilege belonged to a husband. Her conscience spoke up too late. She'd already given Arch permission.

"I'll warn you, when it's tangled like this, it isn't fun to brush."

"Not fun for you..." He let her draw the obvious implication as he lifted the heavy tresses over the chair back.

She straightened her spine, her heart thudding.

"Don't be nervous, sweet pea."

At the endearment, Prudence blushed like a schoolgirl with her first beau. In many ways, Arch was her first. No other man had kissed her or introduced her to passion or stirred emotions buried deep in her heart. Of course, she wouldn't be his first in any sense of the word. He must've left behind a long string of broken hearts, being temptation personified. She had a strong moral backbone and couldn't resist him.

That he appeared to be attracted to her was harder to understand. While she wasn't ugly, she knew full well she wasn't pretty, either. *Plain Prudence*. That's what even her friends had called her. She acknowledged it as a fact rather than an insult. But Arch saw a different woman when he looked at her. He saw a woman who was lovely and alluring. He saw the woman she longed to be.

He lifted a length of hair and began to work his fingers through it. The gentle tugs pulled at her scalp without hurting. "Got to work out these tangles with my fingers before I use the brush, or it'll tear your hair."

"How do you know so much about brushing women's hair?" She tried not to sound jealous.

"When I was four, maybe five, I used to brush out my ma's hair. Hers was long and thick, like yours. Pa wasn't around much to help and I was always underfoot. She must've reckoned a brush would give me something to do."

"My mother used to brush my hair. She didn't worry too much about hurting me, said I needed a tougher hide...like a buffalo."

Arch huffed a laugh. "You can't be related to buffalo. Your hair's too silky."

He dragged the brush through the thick strands. She couldn't call the aching his touch inspired painful. Nothing in her experience had prepared her for this...this craving. While it was too early to name whatever grew between them something more than attraction, they were headed toward a relationship she hadn't thought possible two days ago.

"Where are your parents now?" he asked.

"They're both gone, two years ago this summer, after several years of being bedridden."

"You took care of them."

"As their daughter, yes, it was my responsibility to see to their comfort..." That made it sound like a chore and implied resentment. Even if both were true to some extent, she'd loved her parents and wouldn't have let anyone else care for them. "I did so gladly."

"Taking care of sick folks is hard work."

His reminder humbled her.

"I imagine it wasn't easy taking care of me when I was ill."

"Wasn't as much of a chore as I made out. You aren't old...or frail." His voice dropped lower, the rough tone and his brushing acting like a fine abrasive on her sensitive skin. "I was talking about how hard my ma worked when she had to tend to my grandparents. They were...*incorrigible.*"

She smiled at his clever use of the insult she'd flung at him. "Is that where you get it from?"

"If it means what I think it means, we'd call it *ornery*. My whole family is like that. What about your family?

"I have one brother, Enoch. He's five years older, and he can be *ornery*. Mostly, he thinks he's right about everything. He took his wife and children to California, and he offered to take me along. But...I didn't want to be a burden. I had two younger brothers. Twins. They died when I was eight. I hardly remember them."

"I'd offer to give you two of mine, but you wouldn't want them."

"True," she murmured. "They make you look like a saint. How is it that you turned out so different?"

"My mother let me brush her hair. Kept me out of trouble…"

The gentle, rhythmic brushing lured Prudence into a sensual trance.

Arch smoothed his hand over her head. "How does it feel?"

"Like clay."

"Clay?"

"As in, I'll soon be clay in your hands."

He exhaled a soft laugh. "Oh, I hope so."

His response elicited the thrill inspired when facing danger. Warnings sounded in her head that she dare not let this go too far. "I think you've brushed out all the tangles. There's no need to continue."

"What's wrong? You don't like it?" The brush dug deeper, sliding through her hair, every stroke a caress.

Prudence shivered at a light scrape of bristles against her scalp. *Like it?* If she liked it any more, she would be writhing with delight. A soft sigh escaped from between her lips. "I like it too much."

"Then we'll have to do it every night." His suggestive tone implied more than brushing would be involved.

Her body grew heavy, her limbs refused to move, although fatigue wasn't the problem. Desire made her languid. "Letting you brush my hair every night wouldn't be proper."

"It would be if we—"

Rebel broke into frenzied barking. The dog brushed her skirts as he scrambled from beneath the table and raced outside.

Startled, Prudence jerked up straight. Rebel's barks

broke into long calls. He hadn't barked like that at the Indians. Some danger, or disaster, had arrived. She tamped down a dire premonition. If those were soldiers looking for her, what should she say? "I wonder who's out there."

Arch placed the brush on the table, grumbling. "Whoever it is, I'll send him away." He leaned down and pressed a fierce kiss on her open mouth. "You stay here. We ain't finished."

He'd been about to propose marriage again when the dog went wild. That's what he meant. He never suggested he could love her. She didn't expect to fall in love, either. That didn't mean it couldn't sneak up on her.

Maybe the interruption was a sign that she ought to reconsider leaping *from the frying pan into the fire*, as her mother would've said.

Becoming jittery, she drew her hair over her shoulder and separated it into sections for plaiting. Whoever it was, she couldn't greet them with her hair unbound, looking like a fallen woman—even if that wasn't far from the truth.

A woman's voice called out Arch's name.

Who could that be? A neighbor? He hadn't mentioned any. Perhaps one of her friends had come looking for her. The possibility inspired mixed feelings.

Prudence made quick work of the braid and secured it with the leather tie. Trying to wrap her plaited hair into a bun would be hopeless without hairpins. If the visitor turned out to be no one she knew, she would remain hidden.

She crept to the door and peeked out.

Golden rays slanted across the clearing, illuminating a black buggy hitched to a tired-looking mule. Arch held a woman's hand and supported her arm as she stepped to the ground.

On her spare frame hung a shapeless brown dress and a crocheted black shawl. Her face wasn't visible, being turned to the side and hidden behind a wide-brimmed sunbonnet. At first glance, she didn't resemble any of the women Prudence knew. Tall, but not as tall as Rose; and that plain homespun gown wasn't something Mr. Valentine would allow his Rose to wear, even if she could make it.

Rebel ran in circles around the woman's feet, barking and whining. He darted close, his whole body wriggling with joy. He wasn't upset. He was excited to see her.

The woman spoke to Arch in a voice too low to be overheard. He gave her a hug. The way he put his arms around her bespoke fondness and familiarity.

Jealousy raked Prudence's heart. She exited the open door, raising her hand to shield her eyes from the late afternoon sun. Why, she'd snatch the stranger by her big sunbonnet and tell her to take her hands off...

The woman turned her head. A glimpse of her face revealed too many wrinkles for her to be young. Come to think of it, her shoulders were slightly stooped. Arch had tucked the older woman's hand into the crook of his arm, assisting her in a respectful manner.

Could it be? *His mother?*

Prudence came to a halt, took a step backwards, tempted to turn tail and run. Her face burned, and not from the sun. The tub remained outside, so it was obvious she was staying here and not visiting. His mother must wonder why he had a woman in his house, and what they'd been doing. As if that wasn't apparent. Covering the braid with her hand didn't hide anything.

"Pru, this is my ma, Bessie Childers." With that, Arch confirmed Prudence's fears. "Ma, this is Prudence Walker." He introduced her without explanation. Nothing he added would help matters anyway.

Prudence dipped in an awkward curtsy. "Pleasure to meet you, ma'am."

"Prudence. What a pretty name..."

Was it? No one had ever said so before.

Arch's mother hooked her arm. "Let's go inside and get to know each other while Arch sees to the mule."

Prudence allowed herself to be led along, seeing no polite way to refuse and having lost her chance to sneak out the window and flee into the trees. "May I offer you coffee?"

"I'd be mighty grateful for a cup of tea." Mrs. Childers removed her sunbonnet and smoothed her hand over gray hair braided into a coronet. She hung the yellow bonnet on a peg by the door, indicating she planned to stay awhile. "Sure do hope you don't mind that I came to meet you."

"To meet *me*?" Prudence echoed what she heard, even though it didn't make sense. She searched through the cupboard and took down a tin labeled *Tea*.

"Arch didn't see fit to bring his new wife home. I had to hear the good news from his brother."

Prudence's hand shook as she measured a spoonful of tealeaves into the pot. Good thing she'd turned her back so his mother couldn't see her surprise. Lying wouldn't make things better, but she couldn't come up with a good way to explain the situation either. Not without embarrassing herself and possibly alienating her future mother-in-law by contradicting the tale she'd been told. "Let me put the kettle on to boil while you sit down and rest."

"Thank ye, kindly, Prudence." A creak sounded as Arch's mother sat in one of the rocking chairs by the fireplace. She ran a gnarled hand over the grapevine armrest. "Robert made me a pair of rocking chairs like these when we first got married."

Prudence set the kettle over the hot coals. She had kissed Arch and let him brush her hair, had all but said *yes* to his proposal. Why mention anything, if they would soon be married? Instead, she would use this opportunity to learn more about him. Arch hadn't shared much about his father or his family, other than to say they'd lived over the border in Missouri.

"Arch's father taught him how to make furniture?"

"Oh my, yes. He taught Arch and the boys lots of things, God rest his soul."

"My condolences. How long has Mr. Childers been gone?"

"Eight years this month." His mother's voice grew sad. "Arch was seventeen. The Unionists would've killed him, too, if he'd stayed home. Those days, there weren't a man, young or old, left in McDonald County. They all got killed or run off, or joined an army and fought. Wasn't no middle ground."

The war had ruined so many lives. Which side Arch had chosen as a boy mattered less than what kind of man he'd become. Besides being charming enough to talk a bird off its nest, Arch had proved to be hardworking, generous and honest, when pressed for the truth. He was also surprisingly tenderhearted. His manners weren't polished, and in some cases, his behavior veered into unacceptable, but he was a gentleman in the truest sense of the word.

"Those were terrible times," Prudence agreed. "I'm glad we've put them behind us."

She took the teapot to the table and filled two cups. "There's no fresh milk, I'm sorry…" because she'd used it to make the bread and butter—both of which were inedible. Never again would she waste good food. After she admitted her sin to Arch, she would ask his forgiveness. He had been honest with her, and it was time she was honest with him.

Mrs. Childers lifted the cup and took a sip. "This is fine, honey. Why don't you sit down? You're flitting around worse than a chickadee."

Prudence sank into the other rocking chair, balancing her teacup. "Pardon me, I don't mean to be rude."

"You're not being rude. You're being a good hostess." Mrs. Childers gave her an encouraging smile. "Arch probably told you, he's the youngest of my six boys...four living. When he was a baby, I feared he wouldn't live, either. He was so sickly. Wouldn't think that to look at him now." She chuckled. "He's growed up strong as an oak. Smart, too. I was pleased to hear he found a good woman and settled down."

Prudence drank her tea to avoid responding. Mrs. Childers' assumption wasn't that far from the truth. Best to keep silent.

"There is another reason I stopped by. Arch's brothers went into town three days ago, said they was taking care of the deliveries because Arch was busy with his new wife. Nobody's seen 'em since."

"What were they delivering?" Prudence asked before she realized she ought to know.

Mrs. Childers stopped rocking. "Corn whiskey."

"Whiskey?" Prudence fumbled with her cup. Tea sloshed over the edge and onto the napkin in her lap. "Wh-why were they delivering whiskey?"

His mother looked at her like she might be slow. "They were taking it to the customers."

Prudence forced herself to remain seated. She wanted to jump up and run outside to find Arch and demand he explain why he hadn't told her that his brothers were bootleggers. Now the empty coffin made sense. What better way to transport illegal goods without being suspected?

The rocking chair creaked as his mother put it into motion, expertly cradling the teacup so as not to spill a drop. "Childers make the best whiskey in these parts. Arch's pa learned the secret from his granddaddy, and he taught the boys the trade."

Dear Lord...moonshiners, the whole family...including Arch.

"I'm surprised Arch didn't tell you."

He'd told her he wanted to have his own farm and raise horses. That was his dream. More like a convenient cover. "No, he didn't tell me he makes whiskey."

"Oh, he don't do the distilling. He delivers the whiskey and takes care of the customers. Handles the finances. He's rounded up a good business out here in Kansas." Mrs. Childers spoke with pride, as if bootlegging were an honored profession rather than a scourge on mankind.

Marry a child of the devil and you're going to have problems with your father-in-law.

The old Puritan saying pretty well summed it up. That Arch made moonshine, or sold it, was bad enough. He tempted her to give in to sinful urges. He'd hidden the truth about his livelihood, even after she'd shared her sentiments concerning whiskey. He believed he was above the laws of God and man.

Prudence stared into her cup. Tiny specks swirled in the dark liquid. She didn't have to read tealeaves to know their future. They didn't have one...not together.

The sound of footsteps at the open door drew her attention.

"Sorry it took so long." Arch set a pail along with a slab of bacon on the work surface next to the dry sink. "Thought we might need fresh milk, and we can fry up some bacon..." Their eyes met, and he frowned. "Everything all right?"

No. Things will never be all right.

Prudence balled her fists in her lap, tempted to spew her grief and anger. Lashing out would be pointless, and it wouldn't change anything. She would subdue her emotions, rather than letting them blind her. "We're having a chat, your mother and I."

Mrs. Childers sipped her tea and kept up the slow rocking. That she said nothing could mean she had nothing to say. Or, she'd noticed the thick tension in the room and decided she didn't wish to take a knife to it.

Arch continued to wear a troubled frown as he wiped sweat off his forehead with the back of his hand. After hanging his hat on a wall peg, he stopped by a bucket at the sink, dipped the ladle and took a long drink of water.

He hadn't drilled a well, had to haul in water every day from the spring, and he'd just gotten around to plowing. She had enough knowledge about farming to know corn should've gone in earlier in the month. Maybe he was late because he'd been so busy peddling whiskey.

Why? Why did he have to be a deceitful *bootlegger?*

Pain pierced her heart. The agony worse than what she'd felt when Peter hadn't shown up the day they were to be wed. She'd waited in the parlor, with all her relations and neighbors casting pitying looks her direction, while he had been curled up in a barn, sleeping off drunkenness. Her brother had tried to comfort her by telling her that his childhood friend wasn't worth her tears. Peter had only wanted her because she was a good cook and housekeeper. Little comfort that brought.

In hindsight, she could see that she really hadn't been in love with Peter. She'd been in love with the idea of marriage. This, this wretched longing, dashed hopes and soul splintering pain, *this* was love—and she wanted no part of it.

The creaking stopped. Mrs. Childers set her teacup on the table. "If your wife don't mind, I'd consider it a privilege to make biscuits and gravy to go along with that bacon."

Prudence caught Arch's furtive glance. He might've worried that she had let the cat out of the bag and now he knew. She hadn't disabused his mother of her mistaken notion. He could explain when she was gone.

"That's real nice of you to offer, Ma. You don't mind, do you Pru?"

His hopeful tone and obvious eagerness at the prospect of being well fed intensified Prudence's misery. She also pretended to be someone she wasn't, and resenting him for doing the same smacked of hypocrisy. They had both lied.

"No, of course I don't mind. I'd be glad for your mother to make biscuits. I'm sure they'll be wonderful." Prudence pasted on a smile. She found a bowl below the counter. No need to let on she could make mouthwatering biscuits blindfolded. She would assist his mother and make the job easier on her.

As they worked, Arch whistled that blasted tune, *Dixie*.

Prudence hummed *The Battle Hymn of the Republic*.

This foolishness had gone on long enough. His choices, from songs to careers, proved that Arch was the wrong man for her. She had to get away, as far as possible. Forget about his kisses. Forget how good it felt to be in his arms. Forget that he made her feel beautiful and desirable.

With or without his help, she would get back to town and immediately wire her brother for money to cover her expenses and a one-way train ticket. She'd go to California to live with his family and take care of his children. Be content with the solitary life God had chosen to give her. The Lord couldn't have intended for her to marry a conniving bootlegger.

Arch squatted by the fireplace, adding more hardwood to a low-burning fire. He kept whistling, acting like everything was normal even though he knew it wasn't.

He found Pru's loud humming amusing, but nothing else. The deep flush coloring her face, her tight-lipped expression and stiff posture, it all pointed to her being upset about something. Even her voice had an odd quality, like an eerie calm before the clouds hurled down a blast of rain and hail.

His brothers were missing. Daylight would soon fade, so he would set out in the morning. He had to go look for them, as any responsible brother would, but he hesitated leaving Pru in this predicament. His ma had apologized for disturbing him and his *new bride*. He hadn't corrected her, and it didn't appear Pru had given away the truth, either. Although she'd certainly heard by now the tale his brothers had told. Maybe that's why she was upset.

She appeared content working alongside his ma, following directions without hesitation, being polite and acting interested. With a little training, she'd pick up cooking. She had a quick mind, and he could tell she had more book learning than him. Pru impressed him with her intelligence and educated ways. He knew full well she was better than what he deserved, and he would be proud to have her as his wife.

He rearranged the stack of hardwood then stood and brushed his hands, almost wiping them on his trousers before he recalled the handkerchief in his pocket. He didn't fear her scolding. That's not why he showed good manners. He wanted to make a good impression, so she'd overlook other things about him that didn't quite meet her standards.

She ignored him.

Now wasn't a good time to ask what he'd done. He'd get her alone later and take a walk, find out what bee had crawled up underneath her bonnet and get it out. Kissing her seemed to work before. He'd try it again.

His mind turned to the other problem. The one he'd rather avoid. His brothers must've gotten into trouble, which would come as no surprise. Most times, when they went into town, they found trouble. They drank too much, said the wrong things, picked fights. The last time, he'd bailed them out of jail and promised the authorities that he would keep them out of Centralia. He'd made them swear not to return.

Dang fools.

Glancing over his shoulder, he caught Pru watching him. The hurt in her gaze caught him off guard, like an unexpected punch to the gut. He shook his head, questioning her with his eyes.

Her expression closed up and she turned her back.

That did it. He could handle her being fractious, but he wouldn't let her snub him.

He stalked over and took her by the arm with a firm grip to get her attention. "Come outside with me."

She twisted to look at him and surprise registered on her face. Then her brows slashed down and she planted her feet. "Not now. I'm helping your mother."

"Oh, I'll be fine, honey. You go on with Arch." His Ma barely flicked a look in their direction as she flattened the dough with her hands.

Prudence jerked out of his grasp, snatching up a cloth and wiping flour off her fingers before she marched out the door. He had to clamp his jaw to keep from yelling out. By God, he'd get to the bottom of whatever had her nose twisted out of joint.

She stormed into the clearing, not stopping until she'd reached the edge of the freshly plowed field.

That soil hadn't come up easy, not even with Sophie's help and a freshly sharpened plow blade.

He'd never worked so hard in his life. Carving out a farm and building a dream would take every ounce of strength and determination. He could do it with a wife by his side. But not any wife. Prudence Walker. Who cared if she didn't know how to cook? Anyone could learn that skill. Not every woman had what it took to survive in a land where nature fought against being civilized. Pru would fight back. If he could get her to stop fighting him.

The sun had set the western sky ablaze, turning the tall grass into a red-gold sea that the wind whipped into waves. With every sunset, different colors splashed across the horizon. So much grass would be dreary and uninteresting if not for the breathtaking skies.

Did Pru see the beauty? Did it touch her heart like it touched his? Only the brave—or the foolish—would attempt to tame this land. That was one reason he'd come to Kansas. He loved challenges. Maybe that's why he had his heart set on winning this hardheaded woman who didn't appreciate her own unique beauty.

He approached her from behind and wrapped his arms around her.

She stiffened. "Don't…"

Retreating wasn't an option. He laced his fingers together to let her know he wasn't one to let go easily. "Whatever's bothering you, we can get past it…if we do this together. We can't keep fighting each other."

She placed her hands over his, trying to pry open his interlocked fingers. When she failed, she rested her hands over his. Her rib cage expanded and she released a sigh. "You must let me go, Arch. I cannot marry you. If you're worried about what I'll say to the authorities, you needn't be. I'm leaving. I'll be taking the train to California as soon as I can arrange a ticket."

What she said sank in and triggered a rush of anger. He spun her around to face him, grabbing her shoulders.

"What the dickens are you talking about? You can't go to California. I need you here."

The words were out before he could stop to consider how pathetic the plea made him sound. He *needed* her...and she wanted to go all the way to California to get away from him.

Her eyes grew bright and her nostrils flared like she might start bawling. She turned her face away and blinked fast, regained her composure, which was more than he could say for himself. He'd gotten deluged and couldn't grab ahold of anything to save him from going under.

When had he started needing this woman? He couldn't put his finger on one moment. Desire set in first, and then it grew into something more over lots of little moments. Slipped up on him like a stealthy Indian.

His throat tightened. No way in hell would he lose control in front of her. He spoke low, with an urgent tone to hide the uneven roughness. "When I kissed you, you kissed me back, and it sure didn't feel like a California-here-I-come kiss."

"That was a mistake."

Her cold dismissal of their shared passion drove a knife through his chest. He opened his mouth to demand she take back the lie, and then closed it before he started shouting at her. Losing his temper wouldn't help matters. He'd learned that much by watching his temperamental brothers leave wreckage in their wake.

He took a deep breath to clear his head; couldn't think straight when he got upset or scared, and he was both. Setting his emotions aside, he analyzed the stark misery stamped on her profile. Her lips were pressed into a tight line, her throat worked as she swallowed. She wasn't in control as much as she put on, hadn't turned into a stone statue yet.

Relaxing his grip on her shoulders, he let his hands drift down the back of her arms. Her body swayed toward him, a tiny bit, but enough to convince him she wanted him, no matter if she denied it.

"That kiss wasn't a mistake," he stated, without a shred of doubt. "Something happened to cause you to turn away from me. Tell me what it is. I can fix it."

She backed off, hugging herself. Too unsure or afraid to accept any comfort he might try to give. "You can't fix something that isn't broken. You and your family engage in a business making and selling something I can't abide. I wish you'd told me before."

Arch released a pent-up breath. Although he'd known better than to keep silent, he expected the problem to be something worse. This, he could handle. "You're right, Pru, I should've told you earlier. But it's not a problem like you think. I don't intend to sell whiskey forever, only until I make enough money to get the farm going. That's my plan, like I told you."

She didn't look directly at him or drop her defensive stance, which wasn't a good sign. "If you need more money, you'll sell whiskey again. Or if your family asks for help with the business, you'll give it to them. I don't expect you to change, and you shouldn't for me. You must be yourself, as I must be who I am. We're not alike, Arch. We don't belong together."

Everything inside him denied it. "You're wrong. We got a lot in common."

"Such as?" She turned her head and met his eyes with a challenge. Her boldness fired his blood. He wasn't giving up this strong woman.

"We're both stubborn, and we don't back down from a fight."

"How is that a good thing?"

"If we stop fighting each other and face the world together, nothing can stop us."

Surprise flickered across her face, as if she'd never thought of it that way. But then she went back to hugging herself and hunching her shoulders. "Being hardheaded isn't a reason to get married."

"No? Who else is gonna put up with us?"

They could argue all night or he could do something more effective…and far more enjoyable. Taking ahold of her wrists, he drew her to him, put his arms around her stiff body and held her close. He bent his head and whispered in her ear. "And there's this…"

Her eyes widened with alarm. Without hesitation, without preliminaries, without giving her a chance to come up with an objection, he took her mouth.

For a heartbeat, her lips remained sealed. Then they parted in surrender.

He swept in, desperate to taste her, savoring the unique tang and flavor that was hers alone, inhaling her womanly scent, which mingled with the smell of flour and biscuit dough. His hunger intensified. Not for food. He wanted to feast on Prudence.

She placed her hands on his chest and pressed, a slight resistance, easy to overcome. He deepened the kiss. Teasing. Challenging. Forcing her to duel with him. Submit or engage, she must do one or the other; he wouldn't let her run away.

Her hands fisted and she hammered his chest, tearing her mouth away. "Stop!"

Unwilling to force her, he let her go.

She scrambled backwards, wild-eyed and fearful and breathing heavily. "Stay away from me." She held out her hand like she was warding off the devil.

His heart ached. So did other parts of him. He ached for what she could give him. Even so, he wouldn't use desire to bust down her defenses. That would destroy her spirit.

"Rest easy. I'm not out to steal your soul."

The wind whipped strands of hair across her face. She dragged it out of her eyes and with shaking hands, tried to tuck it behind her ear. "That's not funny, Arch."

"Didn't mean for it to be." He released a heavy sigh. Her objections were a smokescreen to hide the real reason she wanted to turn tail and run. She could be so brave, except for when it came to facing herself.

When she took another step backwards, he stopped advancing. If they kept this up, he would end up backing her into the house. She could retreat, run, or go to California, if she thought it would do her any good. But he refused to let her lie to either of them.

"This thing between us, it's not a mistake, and it won't go away just 'cause you and me don't see eye-to-eye on everything. The problem isn't whiskey, or whatever else you want to put between us. You're running from yourself, Pru."

She smoothed her hair and continued to fight the wind, which seemed as futile as fighting the passion that raged between them. "I'm not running from anything...though I will admit to having a weakness for you."

"A weakness?" He released a humorless laugh. "Is that what you call it?"

She straightened and assumed a prim expression. "That's all it is. That's all it will ever be."

This wasn't the real Pru. He longed to grab her and kiss her until her lips softened and she returned his kisses with equal passion and admitted she burned for him and nothing else mattered. If he did, she'd accuse him of being a scoundrel. Until she accepted herself, she wouldn't accept him.

He lifted his hand in surrender. "All right. You won't have to put up with this *weakness* any longer if you don't want to. I'll take you to town with me when I go to check on my brothers. If you get on a train and go to

California, so be it. I don't want you to leave, but I won't stop you. I'll respect your wishes, whatever you decide."

Chapter Seven

The next morning, Prudence was up before dawn. She hadn't slept a wink, having to share the bed with his mother and being so aware of Arch sleeping on the floor beyond the curtain. If she didn't get away soon, she'd lose the last shred of common sense and marry the scoundrel—and regret it for the rest of her life.

She set off down to the creek with two buckets to get enough water for washing and cooking, while Arch saw to the other chores. The wind had shifted and ominous clouds gathered overhead. Possibly, it would rain about the time they set out. One more thing to dampen her mood further, as if her spirits hadn't fallen low enough.

When it came time to leave, Mrs. Childers hugged her neck and wrapped a shawl around her shoulders. "Looks like it might rain. You ought not go off without a cover. I'll loan you my shawl because you said you didn't have one."

With a stern expression, she addressed her son. "Arch, you go by the mercantile and let Prudence buy some nice fabric, so I can sew pretty things for her.

Shame on you for not taking her shopping before now."

That was the harshest thing Prudence had heard his mother say, and Arch didn't even deserve the scolding. Though he acknowledged it with a silent nod.

Prudence didn't look forward to a long ride ahead.

Arch remained quiet and distant. His somber mood gave her the jitters and added to her doubts about her decision. This morning, she'd half expected him to try to talk her out of leaving. She shouldn't be hurt, or disappointed, having gotten what she wanted. Her freedom.

"You aren't coming along?" she asked his mother.

"Someone needs to stay here and watch over the animals, make sure they'll be here when you get back. Arch can take care of things in town."

Rebel trotted over to the wagon, his tail waving.

Arch shook his head. "Not today, boy. You stay here with Ma."

The dog's head lowered and his tail drooped.

Prudence knelt down and let the dog put his paws on her lap. She rubbed his soft coat, picking out burrs clinging to his fur. She bent her head so Arch wouldn't see her tears. The hound licked her cheeks. "I'll miss you, you old Rebel," she whispered. "Take care of things while I'm gone."

Arch assisted her into the wagon. He didn't say a word until he picked up the reins and called out to Sophie. "Git up!"

After they'd left the farm behind, he guided the wagon onto an unfamiliar path. Worn ruts indicated others used the road, to go where was hard to say. Prudence could see no sign of civilization, not even smoke from a chimney. Hardy grasses grew as high as the side of the wagon and intruded on the road, as if nature intended to obliterate the mark of mankind on its domain. Those intending to tame this wild, remote land would find it difficult, although the effort would be worth it. Maybe that's why Arch had staked out a claim here. He seemed to relish impossible challenges.

Prudence peered at the cloudless sky. Endless blue, like Arch's eyes. Would she ever be able to look up again without thinking about him? She must keep her mind focused on something else. As best she could tell by the position of the sun, they were headed northeast.

Arch hadn't struck up a conversation, not even idle chatter. They had never before lacked for things to talk about. However, she couldn't bear another emotional rehash and suspected he felt the same way, which would account for his silence.

Eventually, they left the grassland and turned onto a road that meandered along next to a line of timber. After some time, the wagon lumbered over a wooden bridge that crossed a creek.

"I don't recall this bridge," she observed.

"You were shut up in a coffin."

"True."

Trying to converse didn't help. He kept his answer short and his attention on the road. The brim of the straw hat cast a shadow over his face, but she could see the fine lines beside his eyes where the skin crinkled when he smiled. He wasn't smiling now. The frown made him look fierce, the way he'd looked the first time she'd seen him and had nearly expired from fear. That was before she'd gotten to know the caring, gentle man.

Before they'd left, he had strapped on his back a sheath holding a knife that had to be close to two feet long. The wooden handle protruded over his shoulder. That wicked weapon gave her the shivers. Was he expecting violence? She knew nothing about illegal whiskey operations, but his profession had to be dangerous and might account for the scars he bore.

She grew more anxious, dwelling on the possibility

of him getting hurt, and needed focus on something else. "How long does it take to get to town?"

"An hour or so, depending on the weather."

An hour away from town all this time. Had she been more diligent, she might've made it back on her own. But then she wouldn't have known the thrill of a real kiss. Her lips tingled as she thought about pressing them to his mouth one last time.

She hugged the shawl and redirected her eyes to the road. No more kissing. No more *thinking* about kissing, either. "The trip seemed much longer on the way out."

"Time passes slower when you're scared."

"I've never thought about it, but you're right."

"About some things I am."

Was that bitterness in his voice? Maybe what he meant was that he had been wrong when it came to her. Perhaps he'd finally opened his eyes and seen the drab old maid everyone else saw. He didn't expound and his staid expression gave her no clue, so she was left to draw her own depressing conclusion.

Looking down at her lap, she examined her work-roughened hands. She had gloves, but rarely wore them except to go out, and hadn't been wearing them when she was abducted. One didn't wear gloves while cooking, or milking cows, or tending to countless other tasks.

Her skin wasn't smooth or ivory white. The sun tanned her before she could finish tying on her bonnet. Brown hair. Brown eyes. What was special about that? Nothing about her inspired men to turn their heads. That's why she hadn't asked for too much—an appreciative husband, hardworking, honest and temperate. Not a man whose kiss made her heart pound and whose touch tempted her to be wanton and heedless…certainly, not a bootlegger. Arch expected too much. He wanted more than she could give.

Tears stung behind her eyelids. She prayed they would soon reach their destination. Before she broke down.

A forlorn whistle sounded from a distance.

At last, Arch guided Sophie onto a wider road where the tracks ran perpendicular. She recognized their location. They were close to town.

She had to gather her belongings and let her friends know she was all right before she bid them adieu, which depressed her almost as much as the thought of never seeing Arch again. "Will you take me to the hotel?"

"Whatever you want." His indifferent response rasped on her nerves.

After she'd rebuffed him last night, he had quit pestering her about marriage, and he hadn't touched her, except to help her into the wagon. He'd been polite and obliging...and she hated it. She missed the rakish rascal.

The hotel came into sight, the first building on the south side of town. As they approached, two soldiers on horseback rode by. The men's eyes followed her with interest.

She tensed. What if they recognized her? She would gain unwanted notoriety sooner than expected. Everyone would be asking her where she'd been and why, and what would she say? That she'd been living with Arch for two weeks? She would be in a worse situation than she'd been after Peter had abandoned her. Alone, unmarried, reviled as a fallen woman.

"Whoa..." Arch pulled the reins. The wagon rolled to a stop next to the plank walkway in front of the two-story farmhouse-turned-hotel.

The skies remained threatening, but thus far no rain, only the incessant wind.

Prudence's heart fluttered like the flag hanging from a pole mounted to the porch support. Breathing became increasingly difficult, as though her windpipe had shrunk. She had an urge to run, but couldn't make her legs move.

She gripped Arch's arm before he could hop out. "Wait…"

"What's wrong?" He studied her face. "You look peaked. Are you ill?"

"No." The answer came out in a whisper. She gasped for air, truly frightened now. "I don't know…what's wrong…"

His brow furrowed with concern. "You were in the sun too long."

She could work out in the sun all day. This had nothing to do with the sun.

"What-what do I say? They'll want to know…what happened."

He glanced over her shoulder at the hotel. She sensed he stalled to consider her question. "Tell them the truth."

The truth would put his brothers behind bars, if they weren't there already. Arch had been willing to marry her to protect them. She couldn't betray him. Especially after she'd promised him she wouldn't. "I can't do that."

The strain on his face softened and his gaze filled with such tenderness she nearly burst into tears. "Here now, if it'll make you feel better, I'll take you to the train station and get you that ticket to California. We can send somebody around to collect your things. You can give me a message for your friends, so they won't worry about you."

She stared, incredulous. The man she'd rejected and hurt had offered to take care of everything so she could leave quickly and be spared humiliation. The obvious motive would be to protect his brothers, except he'd told her to tell the truth.

Prudence slid a furtive look in the direction of the hotel. Leaving without any explanation didn't seem right. However, if she went in there, she had no feasible alibi other than the truth. She could keep her mouth shut and say nothing, put up with the ugly gossip and speculation until her brother arranged for a ticket. Or…

Her heart trembled. Indeed, Arch hadn't been right about everything. She wasn't brave. She was a coward. She'd always known the truth about herself. Now, he would know it, too. "Take me to the station."

Arch didn't hesitate. He picked up the reins and started out for the train station. Sophie's hooves sent dust flying as he guided the horse past wagons lined up for supplies at the mercantile. A few folks stared as they passed. His big horse always attracted attention. He hoped they were looking at the horse, and kept moving.

By God, he would get Pru that ticket and see her safely off, and nobody would stop him.

The soldiers who'd passed by hadn't acted like they recognized her. They'd eyed her like they were imagining her without her clothes on, which had made him madder than a bee-stung bull. He hadn't reacted, even though his fingers had itched to take hold of the Arkansas Toothpick and carve their eyes out.

Rage had struck, unexpected. He wasn't a violent person by nature and rarely needed the knife, although he knew how to use it if necessary. By wearing the weapon, he nurtured a healthy respect, or in his case, a mean reputation. Men gave him a wide berth. Women stayed clear of him. No wonder Pru had rejected him, once she'd learned the truth.

She huddled next to him, wrapped in his mother's shawl, like she was trying to make herself as small as possible to avoid being recognized. She'd panicked at the thought of going into the hotel, facing her friends and dealing with their questions. They would be the kindest. People who didn't know her would spread rumors. She couldn't go for a walk without being pointed out. For a respectable woman like Pru, all the speculating and gossip would be humiliating. Wasn't fair or right, but that's how it was, and she couldn't avoid it no matter what story she gave.

If he had brought her back right off, she wouldn't be ruined. If he hadn't been so danged stubborn and selfish, she wouldn't have to run off to California. She could've stayed and married a man who met her standards. Not an underhanded no-account bootlegger.

People crowded the train station, as usual. He guided Sophie to an open spot in front of the land office next to the ticketing agent. Train schedules would be posted inside. Depending on how long she would have to wait, he could take her somewhere, away from curious stares. He'd search for his brothers after he got her safely away.

"Stay here. Don't talk to anybody. I'll be back with a ticket and we'll find a quiet place to wait."

She offered a grateful smile. "Thank you, Arch. I don't know how I'll repay you."

"Repay me? Pru, you don't owe me anything. But what I owe you can't be counted. Getting you to where you want to go is the least I can do."

He hopped out of the wagon and hurried into the ticket office, not wanting to leave her alone for long with all the folks around. Someone would recognize her and all hell would break loose.

A ticket seemed paltry considering his debt to her. He couldn't fault Pru for refusing him and he would apologize for sulking about it. She had good reasons for hating whiskey and those who sold it to men like the one who'd hurt her. He wished he'd been able to help her get past her doubts and awaken her passionate nature. Another man would get that privilege.

Arch squelched the surge of jealousy. He had no right. He'd never had a right to her.

After he checked the schedule and purchased the ticket, he elbowed his way through the people waiting in line and made it out the door.

Prudence stood by the wagon talking to a man in a black suit and an Army officer. Even from the back, Arch recognized them right off—the railroad agent, Mr. Hardt, and Lieutenant Goldman.

Poor Pru. Her complexion had gone pasty except for two bright spots beneath her cheekbones. She hugged the shawl as if it could somehow shield her. Those men would get the truth out of her, if they hadn't already. Things were about to go from bad to worse.

Arch pushed past strangers and strode over. She wanted to escape, so he'd see to it that she got away.

Pru's eyes widened. "What are you doing?" she asked breathlessly.

She might as well have said she expected him to run. Her low opinion of his integrity withered the remains of his pride. What else would she think, considering how he'd acted thus far? Despite her lack of faith, he'd brazen it out and do his level best to protect her.

"Here's your ticket, Miss Walker."

The railroad agent regarded him with narrowed eyes. Lieutenant Goldman's frown didn't bode well either.

Arch took Pru's hand and stuffed the ticket into it, closing her fingers over it. "The train leaves in two hours. If you'd like, I'll take you back to the hotel to fetch your bags."

The lieutenant blocked his way with a set expression that said it would be unwise to try to push him aside. "A moment, Childers. We'd like a word with you."

Whatever had ahold of Pru's tongue let go.

"Lieutenant Goldman, I told you I'm leaving town. There's no need to bother Mr. Childers. He was getting me a train ticket."

The ache in Arch's chest eased somewhat. She hadn't betrayed him. Maybe she thought it best for her sake to keep quiet. He appreciated her defense, regardless.

"That's right. She's leaving." He let the lieutenant draw his own conclusions because it didn't matter what they were. Once Pru left, the scuttlebutt would die down. Some would wonder why she left, and her friends would miss her. They wouldn't miss her half as much as he would.

The railroad agent glared like he wanted to wrap his fingers around Arch's neck, but it was Prudence he addressed in a tight voice. "Miss Walker, we've been searching for you over the past two weeks. We demand some answers."

Curious onlookers had started to gather. The lieutenant glanced around, finally noticing they were attracting a crowd. He gestured to the building behind them. "Let's step into Mr. Hardt's office. We'll have more privacy."

Pru jerked her chin up and straightened her spine. "I have nothing more to say."

A smile tugged at Arch's lips. This was the Pru he knew, full of spunk and not about to take any guff. His heart filled to the brim with equal parts pride and longing. He wished more than anything that he could be worthy of this brave, beautiful woman. But it was too late to change now, and it was pointless to hope for something that could never be.

The lieutenant eyed Arch with suspicion. "Has this man threatened you?"

"No, of course not," Pru scoffed. "What makes you think that?"

Hardt crossed his arms over his chest. Something

about the smug way the railroad agent looked at him set Arch's nerves on edge.

"His brothers are locked up," the lieutenant answered. "They were bragging to some men in the saloon about stealing brides. When we questioned them, they refused to talk. We need for you to tell us what happened."

Arch kept his expression neutral, holding his surprise inside. So that's what had happened to his stupid brothers. Why hadn't they kept their mouths shut? There would be no talking his way out of this.

Pru's face drained of color. Instinctively, he reached out to steady her. With a gasp, she shrank away like his touch burned her. If she'd slapped him, it couldn't have hurt worse.

Hardt's gaze moved between them, speculative. He'd soon be making assumptions, most of which would be wrong. "Miss Walker, we can delay your departure…until you decide you're ready to talk to us."

These men were treating her like a criminal. Arch curled his hands into fists, prepared to fight for her honor. "You can't hold Miss Walker against her will."

At Pru's gasp, he realized how stupid the reproach sounded coming out of his mouth. He was to blame for her misery. He could think of only one way to make amends.

The lieutenant started to move. Whether he intended to separate them or to take Pru into custody, Arch wouldn't allow it. He pulled Pru behind him, shielding her with his body.

"Here's the truth. My idiot brothers abducted her and brought her to me to be my bride. I kept her with me and tried to talk her into marrying me, but she wouldn't have it, so I brought her back. Now you know where she's been. You don't have to question her or embarrass her any more. It's me you want. Let her go."

Chapter Eight

Prudence watched in shock as the lieutenant led Arch away. Foolish man. He'd lost his mind. She would've kept silent. They couldn't *make* her talk. He should've done the smart thing and slip away while he had the chance, rather than stay and get caught.

The crowd surrounding them moved down the street, following the officer and his prisoner. All males, jostling and snarling, like a pack of dogs. Growing bolder, they began to shout.

"Steal our women, will you? You dirty, thievin' bootlegger…"

"He ravished her! I heard him say so!"

"String 'em up! Them Childers are no good!"

A clod of dirt exploded on the back of Arch's coat.

Horrified, Prudence shouted, "Stop!"

Before she could take a step, the railroad agent restrained her. "Don't even think about getting in the middle of that crowd. You'll cause more problems. The soldiers will take care of it."

Seemingly out of nowhere, blue coats appeared, the

soldiers formed a box around Arch and the lieutenant. Curses heated the air and more dirt clods flew.

Prudence cupped her hand over her mouth to stifle a sob. If the situation turned violent, would the soldiers protect Arch? He hadn't hesitated to protect her. He'd come straight over and had remained by her side, even when it became obvious the lieutenant had set a trap for him. He hadn't even attempted to make excuses. He had sacrificed himself, so she could get away.

Regret didn't begin to describe the emotions welling in her chest. Why hadn't she gotten out of his wagon at the hotel, told him to leave town and not return until she'd gone? She shouldn't have let him accompany her to the station and take the risk.

"Miss Walker?" The railroad agent's concerned frown swam into view. "May I give you a ride to the Lagonda House? The other women would like to see you. They've been worried."

Mr. Hardt's voice sounded odd, almost gentle. Compassion wasn't a trait she associated with him. He put his hand to her elbow.

Prudence shook off the unwanted touch. "Why, now, do you think you have to be nice?"

"If I seemed harsh earlier, I beg your pardon."

"*Seemed* harsh?" She was incredulous. "You *threatened* me. You say you're concerned with seeing the women in your charge happily wed, but all you've done is push us around and bully us. You, Mr. Hardt, are the *harshest* man I've ever met."

The railroad agent weathered the gale with a stoic expression. "Your well-being is my utmost concern, Miss Walker. Pardon me if it appeared otherwise. You'll be free to leave town, if that's what you want, after you talk to Lieutenant Goldman and provide a sworn statement.

She couldn't swear on a Bible and tell a lie, but

113

couldn't betray Arch, either. "I'm not going anywhere until Arch is freed."

"Don't feel too sorry for those men, Miss Walker. What they did was wrong."

What Arch's brothers did was outright criminal. Arch's decisions were misguided. She hadn't suffered during the time she spent with him. For the first time in her life, she'd known desire and true happiness. "Arch protected me."

A raised eyebrow communicated the railroad agent's doubt. "He admitted to holding you against your will. Are you saying he lied?"

"No, but—"

"Then he should be jailed along with his brothers."

"Arch treated me kindly."

"Holding you captive isn't kind."

The truth was more nuanced, although the difference between being captive and captivated would be lost on a hardnosed man like Mr. Hardt.

"He returned me unhurt, so there's no harm done."

"We can't have other men thinking they can steal a woman and hold her hostage if they take a mind to. Releasing the Childers will send the wrong message."

Prudence released a frustrated sigh. "*Blessed are the merciful*. You should consider the beatitude, sir. One day you might need someone to be merciful to you."

"Pru!" The shout came from across of the street.

A petite woman with blond ringlets lifted a frothy yellow skirt and ran toward Prudence, dodging a horse whose rider didn't stop fast enough to suit her.

"Charm!" Prudence rushed into the street to embrace her friend. Charm returned the hug. On her face, joyful surprise mingled with profound relief.

"Thank God, you're all right. What happened? Where have you been?"

Prudence raised her voice to be heard over creaking wheels. "I'm fine, I've been—"

"Get outta the street!"

At the shout, she grabbed Charm and pulled her out of harm's way. A wagon careened past, barely missing them. Another driver coming from the opposite direction cursed and turned his mule team, sending two mounted soldiers onto the sidewalk to avoid a collision.

Prudence linked arms with her friend and ran to the opposite sidewalk, not stopping until they reached the dry goods store. There, they paused, breathing heavily.

Mr. Hardt remained on the other side of the street, watching. The railroad agent could prevent her from leaving town if she refused to make a statement. However, she feared anything she could say might be misconstrued and make matters worse. She didn't know how to help Arch, but her clever friend might.

She leaned down and spoke low, so as not to be overheard by passersby who had nothing better to do than eavesdrop. "Is there somewhere we can go to talk? Somewhere private?"

"The opera house," Charm suggested. "No one's there now but Patrick."

Before Charm had married the owner, the opera house had been a saloon. Prudence wasn't certain about the difference. The establishment served liquor. Had she been with anyone else, she would've suggested another location. But this was Charm, and she wouldn't offend her friend by refusing. Besides, she couldn't ruin her reputation any more than it was already ruined.

They entered through a set of carved doors painted red, a new feature. Prudence had been inside the saloon once, shortly after Charm had married Mr. O'Shea, and then because there was no other way to make amends after a terrible misunderstanding.

The place didn't look much different. The ornate bar

remained, as did shelves lined with colorful bottles filled with whiskey and other noxious spirits. The air smelled of fermented beverages and cigar smoke, the battered tables were now covered with linen tablecloths and fresh sawdust covered the plank floor around spittoons.

Loud pounding came from behind the stage. Mr. O'Shea appeared around a painted canvas he'd nailed to a large frame. The scene showed a castle and courtyard.

"We're putting on a production of *Romeo and Juliet*." Charm explained. She blew her husband a kiss and put her arm around Prudence's waist. "Look who's returned to us, Patrick."

Mr. O'Shea lowered the hammer to his side and took a limping step in their direction. Grievous war injuries didn't seem to slow him down and hadn't stopped him from pursuing the vivacious actress, or from going after her when she'd been coerced to leave town with her crooked manager.

"Miss Walker, good to see you looking well," he said in his Irish brogue.

"Thank you, Mr. O'Shea." Prudence breathed deeply to relieve the ache in her chest. Arch hadn't tried to hold on, he'd made a way for her to leave. One could argue he didn't want her as desperately as Mr. O'Shea had wanted Charm. On the other hand, if he didn't care about her, he wouldn't have given up his freedom to secure hers.

"We'll be upstairs." Charm caught hold of Prudence's hand and pulled her to an open doorway that led to the back room, which was filled with stage props, boxes and more bottles on shelves.

Prudence followed her friend up a flight of stairs, curious in spite of her apprehension. They entered a room that appeared to be the couple's parlor.

Charm shut the door and whirled around. "Now we can speak freely. May I offer you tea?"

Tea sounded nice, but Prudence didn't know how long she had before the lieutenant came looking for her. "Thank you. I don't have time. I need your assistance."

"Have a seat and tell me where you've been." Charm gestured to a sofa. "I'll do anything in my power to help you."

Prudence alighted on the edge of the sofa. She ran her hand over the worn upholstery and looked at the dated, mismatched furnishings. Royal compared to those that filled the cabin where she'd spent the last two weeks. But furniture didn't make a place warm and inviting. She felt more at home in Arch's simple dwelling than anywhere, even her parent's spacious farmhouse.

Charm had to scoot to the end of the cushioned chair to keep from being swallowed. Her toes barely touched the floor. She looked childlike. However, presuming her to be youthfully naïve would be a mistake. Arch looked fearsome, yet he had a tender heart. He could be uncouth and outrageous, but today he'd behaved heroically.

"What's wrong Pru? I've never seen you look so...forlorn."

What could she say? She had condemned Arch for deceiving her. In hindsight, she could see that he'd avoided the truth because he knew it would hurt her and drive a wedge between them. She'd judged him too harshly, and now, it might be too late to make amends.

"Lieutenant Goldman will be looking for me..." Prudence prayed the officer possessed a heart. The railroad agent certainly didn't. "I must give a statement about what happened before I leave town—"

"Leave town?" Her friend's voice rose in an alarmed cry. "Why would you do that?"

"I'm sorry, this isn't coming out right." Prudence pressed her hand to her forehead. "It's all jumbled up in my head..." The more she thought about leaving, the less she wanted to go. She'd miss Charm terribly, and

Arch…she dared not think about how much she would miss him, If she stayed, however, she would face ruin. Worse, she would see Arch around town, and eventually, with a wife. She couldn't bear it. But before she went anywhere, she had to make certain he would be released.

Feeling too warm, Prudence removed the shawl that Mrs. Childers had so graciously loaned her. The poor woman would be distraught to learn her sons had been arrested. In the short time they'd spent together, Prudence had become fond of her. Another person she'd miss. Although Arch's mother might be glad to see her gone. She folded the shawl in her lap, heartsick. "Will you do me a favor and see to it that this shawl gets back to Arch's mother? She's staying at his place."

Charm scrunched her forehead, looking confused. "Why do you have her shawl?" She shook her head. "No, wait. Why were you with Mr. Childers?"

With a deep breath, Prudence launched into the story. She kept the details sparse and didn't mention the kissing parts.

"Oh, my, Pru, what a *dreadful* tale. I'm sure you were horrified. I would've been." Charm leaned forward in her chair, her expression rapt, appearing more intrigued than horrified. "But why did Mr. Childers prevent you from leaving? Is he as corrupt and immoral as everyone says? I must say, when I met him, he didn't act despicable."

Prudence leapt to his defense. "He isn't despicable. Actually, he's very kind. Although he admits he hides his soft heart. After meeting his brothers, I'm sure he does so out of self-preservation. As for why he insisted that I stay, he needs a wife like every other man around here who is trying to secure his land. As well, Arch thought by marrying me he would keep his brothers out of trouble." Her heart nudged, that wasn't the whole story. "I also believe he feared for my reputation. Had I agreed, he would've married me to protect me."

Charm looked doubtful. "Why would a man marry a woman who was foisted off on him if he didn't have some degree of interest?"

"He did express...interest." Prudence averted her eyes from her friend's inquisitive gaze. She couldn't explain why Arch found her attractive, which made her doubt whether what inspired him was real. The illusion might fall away like scales from his eyes. Or he would discover she wasn't the passionate temptress he believed her to be—even if being with him made her feel like one. She had blamed him for corrupting her, when in fact, she hadn't felt corrupt or dirty or any of the things she'd been told she ought to feel. She'd been happier and more content than any time in her whole life.

Her friend regarded her thoughtfully. "You have feelings for him. I can tell. Why aren't you willing to marry Mr. Childers?"

An honest question, and one for which she had an answer, even if it sounded less convincing the more she voiced it. "Because he's a bootlegger. You know how I feel about whiskey."

Charm nodded. "Are you saying he overindulges?"

Prudence gave the question some thought. "No, I don't recall seeing him drink. I presume he does, though."

"If he drank too much whiskey, you'd know, believe me." Charm's tone implied she spoke from personal knowledge.

"Then you understand."

"I understand how hard it is to see someone you love destroy their life. But it doesn't sound like your Mr. Childers drinks too much. What's he like otherwise?"

How did she explain Arch? He wasn't a complicated man. Yet, he had many facets. "He can be very sweet.

He can also be a scamp. He makes me laugh one minute, and the next minute I'm ready to brain him with a frying pan."

"Oh my, yes, I understand exactly what you mean," Charm replied with a laugh. "Sometimes you don't know whether to hug them or strangle them."

"Or kiss them." The remark popped out before Prudence realized what she'd said. She clapped her hand over her mouth—too late.

"Ah, so you kissed Mr. Childers." Charm's amusement turned to speculation.

Prudence straightened her spine. She wouldn't have her friend believe she'd thrown herself at Arch. "Actually, he kissed me."

Charm clapped her hands together, her eyes dancing with glee. "Did he, now? And did you like it?"

Like it? Her lips tingled and her heart raced at the mere memory.

"What kind of question is that?"

"Oh don't look so horrified. You must've liked it a little bit, or you wouldn't be thinking about doing it again."

Prudence huffed to hide her embarrassment. "I wasn't thinking about kissing him."

"Then why did you bring it up?"

"You suggested it."

"No, I didn't mention kissing first. You did."

"Well I…" Prudence stammered, flustered and blushing hotter. "Even if I did, we're not here to talk about…*that*."

Charm's smile grew broad. "Oh, I think *that* is exactly what we need to discuss. If Mr. Childers kissed you it doesn't sound like he's offering marriage purely out of obligation."

Prudence heaved a sigh. Charm wouldn't be dissuaded from this discussion. She might as well have it out, but she couldn't look her friend in the eye while she confessed. "Yes, he kissed me, more than once. He seems to think we're right for each other, though I can't imagine why. We're very different."

"Are you? Based on the way you described him, I think the two of you are more alike than you want to admit. You're letting your strict upbringing hold you back."

The blunt remark came as a shock. Prudence leapt to her own defense. "I won't apologize for having strong beliefs."

"No one is asking you to. But there must be some things that are more important than others. Why do you remain my friend? You denounce whiskey. I think I've even heard you say that acting is the devil's trap."

"I did not!" Prudence drew back, surprised, and then embarrassed, recalling she had voiced something stupid at one point. "All I said was that being an actress could *lead* into the devil's trap. There's a difference."

Her friend's sardonic smile softened. "Oh, Pru, I'm teasing you because you aren't mean-spirited. If you were, I wouldn't like you so much. You care about people. As much as you dislike the liquor we serve, you come here to see me. You remain my friend because you love me."

"What are you saying? That I love Arch?"

"Of course do you. You wouldn't be sitting here, twisting your hands off and talking about kissing him if you didn't."

The truth wrenched Prudence's heart. If she'd dared to acknowledge her feelings earlier, she would've made a different choice. "Even if I do...love him...how does that help get him out of jail?"

Charm tapped her fingers on the bolstered arm of the chair. "If you're his wife, they can't force you to testify against him."

"Truly?" Prudence found it difficult to breath, her heart pounded so hard. Without her testimony against him, the authorities wouldn't have a case. No one could prove she'd been held captive, and if she married Arch, who would care? She couldn't deny being tempted, despite her fears. Arch was good and kind, respectful and caring, protective to the point of sacrifice, and he desired her as much as she desired him. Her face grew warm as she recalled the heat that sparked between them.

He also peddled homebrewed whiskey. His involvement in an illegal trade could prove disastrous for their family, should they be fortunate enough to have children. She would nag because she feared for him. Then, there were his brothers. He would continue to feel responsible, and they would get him into trouble, and she would resent them.

She dropped her face in her hands and shook her head. "Oh, Charm, what do I do? So many things stand between us."

"Do you remember me telling you about Simon, how he tried to ruin Patrick to compel me to go with him?"

Prudence shuddered. "I'll never forget what you told me. That awful man."

"What I didn't tell you was why I went with him in the first place. I didn't want Patrick to pay for my mistakes. I wanted what I sincerely believed was best for him."

Charm's eyes grew bright as she related the story. "Patrick risked everything to come after me. He said there wasn't anything he wouldn't do for me, even if it meant giving up everything he'd worked for. I thought Simon could come between us. Patrick showed me that nothing could stand in our way if we stayed together and loved each other."

Hadn't Arch said something very similar?

"If we face the world together, nothing can stop us."

Inexplicably, Arch desired her. More than that, he saw something in her that he needed—her strength, and of all things, her stubbornness. Together, they could defy impossible obstacles and build the kind of life that would remain a dream otherwise. He knew how much courage it would take for her to remain with him, and how much easier it would be to run away. Yet, he believed in them and in what they could create, together. He'd brought her back to town, not because he didn't need her anymore, but because she hadn't believed.

Chapter Nine

Centralia had an abundance of saloons, a handful of stores, two lawyers and an undertaker. The townsfolk hadn't gotten around to building a jail. Offenders were held in an empty railcar used to transport cattle. Through narrow openings between wooden slats, Arch could see two soldiers assigned to guard the prisoners.

The bluecoats sat on a bench set up beneath a canvas lean-to, which hadn't protected them, or the occupants of the railcar, from sheeting rain blown sideways by the wind. The two soldiers looked as miserable as Arch felt.

He wondered if the storm had delayed Prudence from catching her train yesterday afternoon. He hoped not, despite the fact that his heart ached every time he thought about not seeing her again. Dwelling on his loss made the ache worse, but grief was better than rage. If he let his mind wander to other things, he might start thinking about murdering the men in the railcar with him. Calling them *brothers* was too charitable.

"This place stinks worse'n a pig pen," T.J.

complained. "There's fleas in the straw, and they need to dump that bucket. It's full of shit."

"They cain't hold us here forever," Obe grumbled. "We got rights."

"Rights?" Vern huffed. "What rights, you fool? Cherokee County is under martial law. That means them Yankees can do anything they damn well please. If they want to line us up and shoot us, nobody'll stop 'em."

"Shut yer hole, Vern. We'll get a trial."

"A military trial. Fat lot of good that'll do us."

"They won't shoot us if they want to keep drinkin' our liquor."

Arch clenched his teeth as Obe and Vern went at each other. Again. He put his hands on the rough walls, digging into the narrow openings with dirty fingers, fighting the urge to tear at the boards. The stench and heat were bad enough without having to listen to two braying jackasses.

"Shut up!" He whirled around, glaring at his brothers, who sat together, leaning against the opposite wall.

They stopped bickering long enough to turn baleful looks in his direction.

"Whatever they decide to do to us, we deserve it for what we did to Miss Walker. Her reputation's ruined. She can't hold her head up in town. She's so ashamed she's goin' all the way to California."

Obe unfolded and stood, knitting his heavy brows into a mean scowl, something he did when he wanted to remind his brothers who was in charge. By virtue of his physical strength—his brainpower sure enough wasn't the reason. "All we did was bring her to you. If you didn't want her, you didn't have to keep her."

T.J. nodded in enthusiastic agreement. "Yeah, you should've married the gal. Weren't right what you did, bedding her without wedding her. Ain't proper."

Heat inched up Arch's neck into his face. Even his brothers assumed the worst. Everyone else would, too. Looking back, he could see his foolish plan for fixing things by keeping Pru with him had been out of pure selfishness. He'd wanted her, and so he let himself be blinded to how his actions would bring her harm. He wouldn't disown his responsibility, but he also wouldn't let his brothers squirm out of *their* responsibility for this mess.

"Damn right. I should've brought her back, and let her tell everybody what you did. Let the three of you rot in jail. Then I wouldn't be here, forced to listen to you whine."

"Is that what happened? She blowed on you?" Obe huffed, an arrogant sound of disbelief. "I reckoned that plain old maid would jump at the chance to get hitched. You messed up, not marrying her. Or maybe you don't know how to keep a woman happy."

Arch narrowed his eyes, bringing Obe's bearded face into sharp focus. His oldest brother always could set him off, but he had never come so close to hate. Obe had masterminded the abduction and thought so little of Pru that he imagined she would be grateful. "Don't you speak of her with disrespect."

"I'll speak of her any way I want." Obe rolled up his sleeve, revealing a ropey forearm, and his eyes glinted with anger. "You can try to stop me."

T.J. scooted back, pulling the coats out of the way, presumably to clear a space for the oncoming brawl.

Vern came to his feet and got between them, putting his hands up to keep them apart. "Now simmer down, you two. Ain't the time or place for this."

"Back off, Vernon Lee. You can wipe the brat's nose after I bloody it." Obe rolled up his other sleeve.

After a brief hesitation, Vern finally stepped back. He sent Arch a questioning look, perhaps expecting him to exercise common sense. It was too late for that. He'd stopped being sensible the day he'd met Pru.

Arch braced his feet and flexed his fingers. His tendency to avoid fights had given Obe the idea he couldn't whip his big brother. He'd prefer to make the arrogant cur kneel before Pru, but seeing as she was long gone, he'd have to settle for thrashing Obe in front of the other two. "You'll apologize for what you said, and for what you did to Miss Walker."

His brother's smile broadened. "Make me."

Arch waited too long to throw the first punch. He realized the mistake almost immediately. Not soon enough to avoid his brother's fist. The first blow glanced off his chin and made his teeth snap together. He blocked the next punch. Then he threw his weight and his rage behind a solid blow to Obe's midsection that sent the taller man staggering back against the wall.

A loud crack reverberated, wood splintering. His brother slid to the floor and slumped forward over his knees, groaning. He hugged his middle.

"You broke his ribs," T.J. said in an awed whisper.

That cracking sound couldn't have come from ribs breaking... Or could it?

"He had it coming." Arch spoke with more conviction than he felt. What if he'd dealt his brother a mortal blow? He would never forgive himself, in spite of being angry enough to spit nails.

He eyed the other two, wary of their reaction. Vern and T.J. might decide to take up where Obe had left off. They appeared more concerned about Obadiah.

Arch leaned over and held out his hand, ready to make peace. "Here, let me help you up."

His brother's hand shot out. Before Arch could react, Obe grabbed his wrist and yanked hard, sending him headfirst into the slatted wall. Pain exploded in his head. His vision blurred. Seizing the advantage, his brother threw his weight against him and took him to the floor.

How stupid to fall for the oldest trick in the world.

They grappled as they rolled on damp, filthy straw, both throwing punches, yet not able to get much leverage. In strength, they were evenly matched, but that knock on the head had stunned Arch. His brother rolled him on his back, powerful fingers closed around his throat.

Would Obe strangle him in a fit of rage?

Knowing the answer sent a surge of fear through Arch and he fought wildly to throw off the madman and regain control. Thrashing, he hit something with his foot.

An awful stench filled the air.

"Awww crap," Vern shouted.

"Git up! Yer rollin' in shit!" yelled T.J.

Obe looked away, his grip on Arch's throat lessening. He started to get up. Done with fighting fair, Arch jerked his knee upwards, connecting with the most vulnerable part on a man's body. His brother toppled over with a pain-filled howl, cupping his hands protectively around his balls. He wouldn't be getting up anytime soon.

Arch rolled over, coughing. He couldn't catch his breath because his throat kept closing up from the godawful stench. He crawled away on all fours, as far as he could go. The smell followed him. He tore away his suspenders and ripped off the shirt.

Swearing, T.J. dragged Obe away from the overturned contents of the bucket.

Vern lumbered over to join Arch at the furthest point from the foul mess. He kicked away the stained shirt. "You're both idiots."

True enough.

Arch slumped down and leaned against the wall for support. His body ached in all the places Obe had used him as a punching bag. Threading his fingers through his hair to push it out of his face, he gingerly touched a lump the size of an egg. He couldn't say who'd won, and it didn't matter anyhow. Not much seemed to matter now that Pru was gone.

A noise came from the door, the scraping of the padlock being opened. The soldiers must've heard the commotion and were coming to check on what happened. Good. Opening the door would let in fresh air.

Sunlight spilled into the car and over the soiled straw. The youthful private who entered with a rifle drew back and scrunched his nose. "Good God! What's that smell?"

"I kicked the bucket," Arch drawled.

The soldier didn't smile. Arch thought it was funny as hell. Then again, he found a lot of things funny that no one else seemed to find amusing.

"You don't want to come in here," the private said to someone behind him.

"Yes, we do. The lieutenant gave his permission." The voice Arch recognized, but couldn't place. A moment later, a man in a black suit ducked into the door. The preacher, Stillwater was his name. He must've been sent to give them a chance to confess their sins before a firing squad dispatched them to hell.

"Might want to reconsider holding a prayer meeting in here, Reverend," Arch muttered.

From beneath the brim of a black hat, the preacher took in the scene in one sweeping glance. Didn't even flinch, although his nose had to be rebelling. His gaze came to rest on Arch, and then he pointed and addressed the private. "That man. He's the one we want."

The soldier motioned with his rifle for Arch to get up. Unsmiling, Vern lent a hand. Arch bit back a groan as pain shot through his side. His vision had gotten better, but his head felt like a blacksmith had used it as an anvil.

"What about the rest of us? You can't leave us in here. It ain't human." T.J. scrambled to his feet, apparently ready to abandon Obe, who remained curled up on the straw, clutching his balls and moaning.

"You three, stay." The private raised his rifle to emphasize his point.

What purpose the preacher had with him, Arch couldn't fathom, but he gladly followed the reverend out the door and away from the smell.

The bright light outside momentarily blinded him. Dizziness struck. He held onto the metal rail so he didn't fall off the last step.

"Arch?"

He froze at a voice he thought he'd never hear again. Then he staggered, finding the ground with his foot a moment before he lost his balance.

Pru appeared in front of him. She'd changed into a brown dress with a cheerful smattering of white and yellow flowers. Perched on her head was a little straw hat with what looked like turkey feathers. Dark curls framed her face.

She looked fresh and young and so pretty it made his heart ache. That knock on the head might've done something to his brain, and that was why he *thought* he saw Pru all dressed up like she was going to church.

The fantasy woman drew closer and touched his cheek. The contact jolted through him.

Good God, she wasn't a dream. She was real.

A throbbing beat in his chest became a wild drumming. He had to moisten his swollen lip before he could speak, and even then, his voice came out sounding like a file on metal. "What are you doin' here?"

Her nostrils flared as if she'd picked up his scent and distress clouded her gaze, which was completely understandable. "I've come to marry you."

Chapter Ten

The wedding took place an hour later in the railroad agent's office. When Prudence saw Arch again, he had cleaned up…somewhat. He wore a fresh shirt, likely borrowed, had slicked his hair back and washed his face and hands. Bruises marred his chin and cheekbone, and he had a cut on his lip. He hadn't shed light on what happened to him, and there wasn't time to talk before the ceremony began.

When they stood together before the preacher and began to say their vows, tears sprang to her eyes. She tried to stop them, but couldn't, and blubbered throughout the entire ceremony. Every time she looked at Arch, a fresh flow would start. When they left, she was crying.

Embarrassed by her loss of control, she didn't open her mouth until he helped her into the wagon and took up the reins to turn the horse homeward.

"I'm sorry I turned into a watering pot." She mopped her eyes with a handkerchief.

"You all right now?"

"I believe so."

"That's good." Relief flickered in his clear gaze and the tightness around his mouth eased. Like most men, he didn't understand happy tears and had no idea what to do with a weepy woman. At one point, he'd stopped the ceremony. Her assurances hadn't seemed to entirely convince him, but he'd let the reverend continue.

"Honestly, I don't know what came over me. I'm usually not so teary. I suppose it can be forgiven on my wedding day."

He eyed her with solemn speculation. She hoped he might make a joke to ease the strain, but he remained quiet. Not even a wisecrack when he had secured two absurdly heavy steamer trunks in the back of the wagon. Most of what she'd packed was her mother's china and her father's favorite books. At one time, those belongings had been the most important things in her life. That was before she'd met Arch. He had given her something she couldn't put a price on or pack away. She hadn't imagined she could find a treasure as rare as love, until he had fanned the flames. If only she could be sure he wanted this marriage as much as she did.

She expected him to be glad that she'd decided to stay, and had hoped he would be pleased about her decision to marry him. He appeared to be neither.

"Don't be a stranger," Charm called out, waving as the wagon pulled way. She'd stood beside Pru, along with three other friends. Patrick O'Shea had acted as best man after Arch refused the lieutenant's offer to bring his brothers to stand beside him.

"We'll miss you!" Delilah held up a lacy handkerchief. Her cheeks were wet, which was nothing unusual. She cried at the drop of a hat.

Susannah Braddock's seven-year-old son chased after the wagon, yelling. "Bring an apple pie when you come back."

Prudence grimaced at Arch's stony expression. He

probably thought her pies tasted as bad as her beans. Hopefully, he wouldn't be too angry when she confessed her deception. An apple pie might be just the thing to make the truth go down easier.

She turned and waved at her friends. "Thank you for everything! I'll be back to visit!"

Chances were good the others would be married by then. They would've all been married weeks ago, if Mr. Hardt had gotten his way. Thank goodness that hadn't happened. Prudence was certain she wouldn't be married to Arch. She had been ready to settle for some staid farmer closer to her age. Instead, she'd risked her heart and married a man five years younger, who happened to be a bootlegger, a man with an uncertain future. But he was the man she loved. Deep inside, she knew she'd done the right thing. She wasn't sure she had done the right thing soon enough.

Her mood drooped lower than the feather dangling in front of her face. She flicked it out of the way and tipped the straw hat forward. The brim barely shaded her eyes. "I don't know why I let Susannah talk me into wearing this fancy hat. A sunbonnet would be much more practical."

Arch darted a look at her frivolous purchase. "The hat suits you..." His gaze held her eyes a moment before sliding downward. "And the dress."

Her skin warmed beneath his scrutiny. "Gray is easier to keep clean. But I thought the calico more appropriate for our wedding." She brushed dust off her skirts and tried to lighten the mood. "Susannah also pointed out, this is the one dress I own that's in a cheerful color."

"We could go back and see about purchasing some fabric so Ma could make you another dress. I forgot about it."

"Heavens, no. Don't turn around." She didn't want him to feel guilty. "I don't need more fabric at the moment. When I do, I can sew my own things. Your mother doesn't have to sew for me."

"She'll insist on making you something, so you might as well let her."

"Are you saying she's as stubborn as I am?" Prudence smiled, thinking he'd be amused if she poked fun at herself.

"Hard to say which one of you I'd wager on." He didn't smile, but at least she'd gotten him to engage in wry banter. His somber mood might have nothing to do with her.

"Are you sure you're not in pain?" She reached over and lightly brushed her fingers along his jaw where a bruise had turned his skin dark purple.

He turned his head to look at her and dismay filled his gaze.

The side of the wagon dropped. Her heart stopped as she felt her backside leave the seat. She grasped the rail to keep from flying off and bounced as Arch hauled on the reins.

"Haw," he called out. The horse veered to the left, bringing the wagon out of the gully on the right. The wheels bumped and then the ride became smooth again.

Arch directed a frown at the road.

The quivers in her stomach worsened when she looked back at where the wheels had carved deep ruts into the mud. He hadn't noticed that place where the road had been washed away. She must've startled him, or maybe hurt a sore spot, or he hadn't wanted her to touch him. No, she couldn't read too much into his dismayed reaction. These past two days had been difficult.

"I'm sorry, I didn't mean to distract you. What happened?"

His frown deepened. "Got into a disagreement with Obe."

Obe. That was his eldest brother, the one that reminded her of a dyspeptic grizzly bear. What had the foul-tempered creature done? Broken a chamber pot over Arch's head? The poor man stunk like an outhouse when they'd hauled him out of that railcar.

"More than a disagreement, I'd say."

Arch flicked a sharp look that was hard to read. "He disrespected you."

"You fought over me?" The knots in her stomach tightened.

"As well over you as something else. Obe's had a chip on his shoulder for years. I didn't see a need to knock it off—until now."

The very last thing she wanted was to come between him and his family. He might be angry with them now, but eventually he'd resent her for being the wedge. Despite how his brothers had treated her, despite her aversion to their way of life, she had to build a bridge or ill feelings would swamp her marriage.

"I pleaded with the lieutenant for leniency. He assured me your brothers would be treated fairly. I wish I could've done more, but Mr. Hardt is adamant about setting an example, and I think he's influenced the lieutenant's decision. We can appeal, I'm sure."

Prudence clasped her hands together but refrained from wringing them. She refused to second-guess her decision. Even if Arch had changed his mind about wanting her and married her to avoid spending time in jail. After all, someone needed to take care of his brothers' families and his mother if the other men were detained for any length of time. Arch would see that as his responsibility. She would help him, and time would heal the rift between them. She had to be patient.

The wagon rumbled along the road. To keep her mind off miserable thoughts, Prudence memorized landmarks: an old oak tree at the place where they turned away from the railroad tracks; the bridge across the creek before they reached the path where the grass grew as tall as the wagon bed.

"I should able to find my way to town easy enough."

Arch looked at her askance. "Do you plan to leave?"

"Leave?" He didn't mean for good. Or maybe he did. She released a laugh to ease the tension. "I won't right away, but I expect I'll need to go to town at some point. If you'd rather I not go alone, I can wait until you're ready."

The wind picked up seemingly out of nowhere, bending the grass and setting the few trees into motion. Prudence held onto her hat. Charm had helped her arrange her hair in attractive curls around her face for the wedding. Now all that effort would be ruined. The fancy style wasn't practical, anyway, and she was nothing, if not practical.

She had set her foot on this path. Whether marriage led to disappointment or happiness depended on her. Somehow, she would find a way to break through the barrier Arch had erected.

As they approached the house, Rebel rushed out to greet them. The dog barked and circled as Arch lifted her from the wagon and set her on the ground. The sadness in his gaze sent her heart reeling.

Her breath snagged on a sob, but she swallowed her tears. This foolish crying had to stop. Until she'd gotten the silly notion into her head about winning his love, she had never expected it. Her goal had been to find a husband who would appreciate her. The man she'd married would appreciate her a great deal more if she wouldn't burst into tears every time he looked at her.

"Arch! Prudence!" His mother came out of the house and rushed over to embrace them. She took a good look at her son's face and frowned. "What happened to you?"

"Got into a fight," he said flatly. "With Obe."

Mrs. Childers shook her head in reproach. "You know better than to tangle with a bear."

"The bear got what was coming to him." Arch showed no sign of regret.

Prudence gnawed her lip, wondering if Arch would admit to *why* he'd fought with his brother.

"Where are they?" Mrs. Childers asked.

"Locked up in a rail car until the army decides what to do with them."

Her jaw came unhinged. "Because of a fight?"

"No, the fight happened later. They got arrested for stealing Pru. Two weeks ago, they tied her up and brought her out here, said they'd done it so I could have a bride. Then the fools went and bragged about stealing a woman. When I took her into town, the lieutenant locked me up with them. She got me released by marrying me."

The fragmented explanation served to confuse his poor mother even more. She kept shaking her head with her mouth hanging open. "Well, I never... Why would they...? And you two got..." Her questioning gaze moved to Prudence. "Married?"

Caught in the limelight, Prudence felt her face heat up. Her lips sealed like melted wax.

Arch put his arm around her waist and pulled her against him as if they were already familiar, which made it look worse. "Pru didn't do anything wrong, Ma. She tried to leave before but I wouldn't let her."

His confession jerked her out of her daze. Whether he wanted this marriage or not, he wouldn't spurn what he viewed as his responsibility. However, she refused to let him make it sound as if he'd forced her to take him. "Arch didn't make me do anything I didn't want to do."

He glanced at her questioningly, but then turned to unloading the wagon.

His mother recovered from her surprise. "You two must be hungry. I'll get some dinner on the table."

"I'll give you a hand." Prudence's worries multiplied as she imagined what might be going through her mother-in-law's mind. Mrs. Childers couldn't be happy finding out that she'd been lied to and that Arch's brothers were imprisoned. The difficult situation would be made worse the longer the men were in jail.

Arch carried the trunks inside, one after the other, and then went back out to unhitch the horse. Rebel trotted after him. Abandoned by both, Prudence felt even more alone. She considered going after him and taking him aside privately. He might respond better to an affectionate touch if he didn't have to focus on driving a wagon. However, she couldn't walk off after telling his mother she would help prepare dinner, and she had some explaining to do.

"I'm so sorry about what happened."

His mother went straight to the fireplace. "Don't sound to me like you got anything to be sorry about."

"We should've told you the truth sooner."

Mrs. Childers used a thick cloth to remove a Dutch oven nestled among the smoking coals. She lifted the lid and the smell of freshly baked bread filled the air. "Bread's ready. I'll get the stew."

Prudence decided to drop the subject of apologies for the time being. The best peace offering would be to provide help with dinner. Plus, it would give her a chance to show Arch she wasn't worthless in the kitchen. "Why don't I make a pie or cobbler?"

"No need. I can put something together real quick. You sit down and rest."

"Thank you, but I can't sit. I need to keep busy." Prudence went to the flour bin. She wanted to be of help. She wanted Arch to be glad he married her. How could she earn his appreciation, much less his love, if she loafed around and let his mother do all the work? "All I need is vinegar, butter, sugar and eggs. I can whip up a vinegar pie in no time."

"That'll suit Arch. He loves vinegar pie." His mother set an iron pot over the hot coals and picked up a long wooden spoon.

"What are some of his other favorites?" Prudence would make sure she knew, so she could surprise him and cook them.

"Blackberry cobbler, peach cobbler, raisin pie… Put sugar in anything and he'll be happy. He has a fearsome sweet tooth."

"He doesn't know I can cook," Prudence admitted. Might as well come clean. "You see, at first, I was frightened…"

"Imagine so. Who wouldn't be?"

"I thought if I could convince him that I would make a terrible wife, he'd return me. So I scalded the butter, burned the bread and put soap into the beans."

"Soap?" His mother laughed. "So that's why he's so eager for me to cook."

"I wish I hadn't deceived him." Prudence heaved a sigh. "I wish I'd handled things differently."

"Wishing won't change anything. Sounds like you two need to have a long talk."

After preparing the pie, Prudence took a seat at the table to wait for it to bake. His mother had it right. Her mother would've advised the same. Hard as it might be to hear Arch tell her he wasn't sure about his feelings toward her, if he had doubts, she needed to hear them.

Mrs. Childers finished warming the stew. Her mood appeared thoughtful, almost pensive. She had to be worried about her sons being imprisoned and their future uncertain, or she might have questions about the odd circumstances surrounding her youngest son's marriage. Possibly, she needed something more done. Prudence hoped for the latter, as she found it easier to tend to tasks than to engage in difficult discussions.

"Is there something more I can do?"

"Other than wait on that pie to cook?" Mrs. Childers said, wiping her hands on her apron. Her gaze rested on Prudence, turning speculative. "Honey, I ain't one to pry, but there is something I'd like to ask."

Prudence tensed. Some subjects she'd rather not discuss. However, she needed to hear whatever his mother had to say if she hoped to restore and deepen their relationship. "Ask anything."

"Why did you marry my boy?"

That was the easiest question.

"I love him."

His mother nodded, as if the answer didn't surprise her. "You ought to tell him."

Hadn't she?

No. Not in so many words.

He hadn't mentioned love, either. If she declared her love and he didn't return her deep feelings, his rejection would crush her. Didn't Arch deserve to know, regardless?

Mrs. Childers retrieved an empty bucket by the sink and held it out. "You want to do something helpful? Go down to the spring and fetch us some water."

Prudence noticed a second full bucket. That water looked fresh. His mother was giving her an opportunity to talk to Arch, alone. What a dear, wise woman.

"Thank you," she said, and took the handle.

Chapter Eleven

*A*rch released the mare into the pasture. Soon as he'd shut the gate, he headed down the path toward the creek. Before the wedding, he had washed off the worst of the stench and had borrowed a fresh shirt, but he didn't feel clean. Prudence hadn't mentioned anything, but her eyes kept watering.

He could get rid of the smell, but he couldn't wash away all the things about him that offended her. For a brief while after she announced her intention to marry him and the soldiers escorted him away to get cleaned up, he'd been deliriously happy. He'd supposed she had changed her mind because she decided she couldn't live without him. That delusion ended when the lieutenant told him he owed it to his wife to stay out of trouble, considering her *sacrifice*.

His worst fears were confirmed after he joined her in the land office and she bawled throughout the wedding ceremony. Knowing he was the cause of her misery hurt worse than getting his head bashed. He stopped the ceremony to give her a chance to back out. She didn't take it and he couldn't shame her by refusing to marry her. Not after she went to so much trouble to save his sorry hide.

Upon reaching the creek, he stripped off his clothes, tossed them over a bush, and waded into waist-deep water. His skin pebbled from the cold, but the water felt good with the air being so hot and humid. He rubbed a ball of soap over his chest. Felt bad that he'd showed up at his wedding smelling like an outhouse. Prudence deserved better than a hurried ceremony with a stinky groom. He'd find some way to make it up to her.

A squirrel dashed into the bushes. Rebel barked and chased after the critter. The squirrel scrambled up a nearby trunk and then leapt from tree to tree. Rustling sounds and trembling leaves in the bushes gave away the dog's position. Rebel couldn't earn his keep as a hunting dog anymore. Didn't mean he wouldn't try. A good lesson, maybe?

Arch scrubbed his hair, ruminating. Pru had a soft spot for a lame dog that wouldn't give up. Could she love a bootlegger who might not ever amount to much, no matter how hard he worked?

He rinsed his hair and sluiced off the water. Soapy bubbles clung to leaves and swirled downstream. Wasn't as easy to wash away the guilt. He'd been eaten up with it ever since leaving that office with his new wife on his arm. He'd got what he wanted—and it had cost Pru her principles and the future she might've had with a better man.

She thought it was her fault he got locked up, and she wasn't the type to walk away. Regardless, she must have some feelings for him. She wouldn't marry a man she didn't care for. That didn't mean she loved him, or would ever love him. She might even come to despise him.

After he told her the bad news, what he had to do,

she might decide she wanted to go to California after all.

Prudence followed the sound of barking down the path that led to the creek. Rebel stayed near Arch when he wasn't with her.

Two squirrels balanced a low limb scolded her, or maybe they were fussing at the dog. He loved to chase squirrels and rabbits even if he no longer had any hope of catching one.

Rebel rushed up to her, his tail wagging and his tongue hanging out as he panted with obvious satisfaction.

She leaned over and rubbed his head. "You are a dirty mess. Come with me and let's get you cleaned up for dinner. I don't know what Arch is thinking to let you come in the house smelling so bad. His nose isn't as keen as yours. He needs a bath, too."

Sounds of rushing water came from behind the bushes. A flash of white and brown over a sumac caught her eye. Those clothes belonged to Arch.

The dog gleefully sounded a call and bounded off.

"Rebel!" Arch's shout came from the direction of the creek. "Stop that racket! What d'you got there? You done chased all the squirrels into the trees."

Prudence jerked to a halt. What should she do? Run? Stay? Call out so he'd know he wasn't alone? Rational thought scattered as the bushes parted and out stepped Arch without a stitch on.

A gasp lodged in her chest, as she took in all at once her husband's tanned, muscular body made more magnificent sheened by water.

The bucket thudded as it hit the ground.

She ought to avert her eyes, but not for all the tea in China could she tear her gaze away.

He appeared equally surprised and didn't move from his frozen position.

Over the course of thirty years, she had seen few men undressed: her father when he'd been sick and old and needed taking care of and Peter, whom she'd caught skinny-dipping with her brother when she was little more than a child. They looked nothing like her husband.

Light and shadow played across Arch's broad shoulders and chest. Muscled ridges crossed a line of dark brown hair pointed like an arrow down his abdomen. His legs weren't at all skinny, and his…private part…was much larger.

"Oh my." The whispered words came out with her breath.

He made a grab for the trousers. His sharp movement broke her trance and she turned her back to give him privacy. She raised her hands to her face, her fingers cold against her hot cheeks. What on earth had she been thinking to stand there and stare at him?

"Pru?"

The soft rustling conveyed he was putting on his clothes. A very wanton part of her wished he'd leave them off. "Is everything all right?"

What a question. He was oh-so-very *all right*. Perfect was the word that came to mind.

"Your mother sent me for water." She motioned at the bucket that had fallen over when she dropped it. "I'm sorry for surprising you. I should've called out."

"No reason to be sorry. We're married now. That means we got a right to look." His voice hinted at amusement.

Her face blistered from the heat. Of course he'd noticed her gawking. Embarrassment caused her to respond in a sharper tone than intended. "Even married people don't prance around in front of each other unclothed."

"They don't?" He covered her shoulders with his hands. His touch penetrated her dress and the warmth settled in a low spot between her legs. The same response she had whenever he held her and kissed her. The heat would quickly turn to a needy ache.

He brought his lips near her ear. "Perhaps you ought to teach me then, about what married folks do."

Her heart constricted painfully. She knew nothing about being married, as he was well aware. "Don't tease me...not about this."

He sighed into her ear, making her shiver. "Sweet woman, you ought to know by now what I sound like when I'm teasing, and when I'm dead serious..." He brushed a kiss on her neck. She felt it clear to her toes. "Teach me Pru. Show me how to be the kind of husband you want."

His low voice reverberated, setting off flutters in her chest. As he'd suggested, his tone held no trace of humor. Strangely enough, he sounded anxious almost pleading. Not like a man who didn't wish to be her husband.

She'd misread his earlier mood, misunderstood why he'd been upset. She had misjudged a great many things, most of all herself.

Her upbringing, as her name suggested, had schooled her to be prudent. With Arch, she was anything but prudent. With him, she'd become a reckless woman who took chances she had never dreamed she would take. With Arch, she could be her true self instead of the person others expected her to be. With her husband, her spirit could soar like the wild hawks that circled high above the tall grass.

"You've taught me far more than I could teach you. Let me show you what you've taught me..." Turning, she looped an arm around his neck and pulled his head down for a kiss.

145

Their lips melded as if they'd been made to fit together. Kissing him came as natural as breathing. His arms went around her waist and he pulled her closer. She slipped her free hand between them and with her fingertips learned the shape and textures of his lightly furred chest. His muscles tightened beneath her touch, signaling the effect she had on him. Perhaps more than she'd realized.

She took the initiative and deepened the kiss.

His eager response fueled her courage and fanned her desire into a roaring blaze. She slid her hand lower on his stomach, slipped her thumb beneath the waistband of his trousers, encountered the top button and flipped it open.

He groaned into her mouth. His hands, having made several trips over her back, moved up her arms and his fingers closed in a tight grip. Did that mean he wanted her to stop, or continue?

Her heart trembled from wanting him so desperately. More than that, she wanted to show him how perfect he was, just as he was. Thus far, she had followed her instincts, but she'd ventured into deep water and didn't know how to swim. He might expect she did, considering her boldness. She'd make a fool of herself if she didn't slow down and let him guide her.

"This is all I've learned…so far. Will you teach me more? Show me how to please you?"

He pressed a tender kiss on her mouth. "Aw Pru, you please me just by breathing."

His heavy-lidded eyes darkened with desire and something more, something so infinitely sweet and gentle it put a lump in her throat.

Before they dove into the depths together, before he taught her all the things she'd wondered about and longed for, she had to tell him what he meant to her. He deserved to know he owned her heart before she gave him her body.

"I love you, Arch. Teach me how to show you."

Loving Pru in the shade beside the creek, on a bed made from his rumpled clothing, proved far better than any fantasy Arch could've dreamed up. He shifted his arm beneath her neck to make her more comfortable. Her eyes were closed and she had a sweet, satisfied smile on her face, as he imagined Eve must've looked lying naked and flushed with pleasure in Adam's arms.

He could hardly believe his wife had been so bold as to come to him. Even more unbelievable, she'd fallen in love with him. Made no sense. Then again, much of creation didn't make sense but that didn't mean it was any less miraculous.

Together, they'd found Paradise. It couldn't last any more than it had all those eons ago. But for a little while longer, he wanted to linger and pretend he'd done nothing wrong. The illusion would be over as soon as he gave her the bad news.

Leaning over, he kissed the tip of her nose. "What are you dreaming about?"

Her eyes remained closed, but her smile broadened. "You."

"What am I doing…in your dream?"

"Loving me," she whispered.

"Like this?" He caressed her breasts with his free hand. She had a body made for loving, all curves and softness and smooth skin that turned rosy when she was aroused.

Her eyes fluttered open, wide with surprise. "Y-yes…something like that."

"Let me know if there's a part I missed." He continued the exploration with his lips.

"Oh!" Her fingers plunged into his hair, drawing him closer. He gladly fulfilled her request for more attention. She'd alternately stroked and fondled and even pulled his hair while he'd loved on her. Her touch, however soft or painful, excited him beyond all measure.

Her breathing grew ragged. Soon, she'd start making those adorable mewling sounds in the back of her throat.

A real gentleman, like what she deserved, wouldn't have taken all her sweet affection while letting her believe that he could give her the kind of life he'd promised. She claimed she loved him, but she might not realize what loving him would require. With a groan, he came to his hands and knees, putting a stop to their play.

Her pretty brown eyes shone with confusion. "What's wrong?"

"We got to talk…"

"Right now?" Her gaze moved down his chest and lower to where his John Henry stood at attention. At the questioning look she gave him, he released a rough laugh.

"Bad timing, I know…" He got up and fetched his trousers. "Might be less distracting if we get dressed."

As she pulled on her shift, she cast furtive glances out of the side of her eyes. He'd finished dressing before she started fastening the stays on her corset. By the time she got to the dress, he couldn't wait any longer and took over the job of slipping the smooth white buttons into the buttonholes.

"Thank you." Smiling, she reached up and took his hands.

He gathered her fingers and brought them to his lips, and the words in his heart spilled out. "You're the best thing that's ever happened to me."

She cast her eyes downward, smiling shyly, like a

young woman receiving her first compliment from a man. "I feel the same way."

He longed to shower her with compliments to make up for all the ones she'd missed. That would send them off on another detour. Later, there would be time, God willing. "You might not feel so charitable after I make a confession."

"You have something to confess?" Worry flickered through her eyes, although her gaze remained steady.

He would rather cut out his heart than disappoint her. Yet, he couldn't avoid it. The right way to do this, give her the truth without trying to put a shine on the apple. "There's no telling how long my brothers might be in jail. I'm done with trying to help them, but I can't turn my back on their families. They got wives and children that depend on what we make from selling moonshine."

With a thoughtful expression, she drew the hair he'd loosened over one shoulder and nimbly wove a soft-looking braid. "I was afraid that might be the case…"

"It's not bootlegging I'm talking about. I have to go back and run the stills. That means I can't stay here and be a farmer and raise horses like I promised. Not now, anyway. Maybe not ever…" He flexed his hands rather than taking hold of her hair, or worse, dragging her to him and clinging to her. If he tried to hold on, knowing how she felt about how he made a living, she would eventually grow to despise him. She deserved a better life. She deserved a better man.

"I should've told you earlier…instead of letting you think everything was going to be like I said. If you don't want to stay with me, I understand."

The color drained from his wife's face. Her expression froze in a look of disbelief. "What are you saying? You don't want me to stay?"

The hurt in her voice ripped out his heart. "Of course I do. There's nothing I want more. But I love you, Pru.

That's why I want you to be with a man you'll be proud of. Someone who can give you the kind of life you deserve."

She blinked as if what he'd said astounded her. Then she threw her arms around his neck. "Oh, Arch, I love you…and I'm proud of you no matter what you have to do…and there isn't any other life I'd rather have than one with you."

The rush of relief left him trembling. He caught her against him in a tight embrace. "You better be sure. Because I won't ever let you go again."

"I've never been so sure of anything in my life." She reached up and cupped his cheek. Her dark eyes flashed with determination. "You told me once that if we faced the world together, nothing could stop us. I believe that, Arch."

Looking at his brave, beautiful wife, he believed it, too. He cupped her cheek and bent to seal their commitment.

A bark interrupted their kiss. Rebel stuck his nose in between them, making himself a nuisance.

Arch stopped kissing Pru long enough to acknowledge the jealous hound. "Sorry, old soldier. She likes my kisses better."

"He's telling us dinner is ready." Pru heaved a reluctant sigh. "We'd better get back."

Upon entering the house, a delicious smell greeted them. Arch's stomach started growling. He went directly to the table and leaned over a pie, breathing in the heavenly smell. "Mm, vinegar pie, one of my favorites. Thanks, Ma."

"Don't thank me, thank your wife. She's the one who made it." His ma replied, dishing stew into bowls.

Arch kept the smile glued to his face as he looked at his wife. "Did Ma help you?"

"Not a bit," his mother interjected. "She done it all by

herself. Wouldn't take any instruction. Said she wanted to surprise you."

Pru fairly glowed with pride. "Go ahead, cut yourself a piece. I'm eager for you to taste it."

His stomach knotted in protest. Thinking about how bad her last meal had tasted made his throat close up. He took a knife and cut a thin slice, wouldn't hurt her feelings, even if it killed him.

He took a bite. Flaky, sweet, slightly tart... *Delicious.* Relieved and thrilled, he finished off the first slice and cut another. "You did real good, Pru."

"I'm glad you like it."

"Will you make another one?" Could be her one edible dish was vinegar pie. He could live on that.

"I'll make whatever you like." She twisted her fingers together in front of her, nervous. His mother went about her business, putting dinner on the table, pretending to ignore them. His instincts kicked in and told him something odd was going on.

"Arch, I have a confession..."

He polished off the second piece and licked his fingers.

"I ruined the butter and overcooked the bread and put lye soap in the beans...on purpose."

He should've known, given how clever she could be. Sometimes she was too smart for her own good. Based on her anxiousness, she thought he'd be angry. He wasn't, but he couldn't resist having a little fun. "You tried to poison me?"

She turned a little pale and wrung her hands. "No, no I never intended that. You can't believe I would knowingly do you harm."

He arched an eyebrow, telling her without words he thought her capable of villainous intent.

"Perhaps I-I wanted to give you a stomachache, but nothing more." She pleaded with her eyes. "I'll make it up to you, I promise. I'm a very good cook. I can fix all your favorites."

"All my favorites?"

"Gladly."

Now they were getting somewhere. "That'll involve more than cooking."

Seeing awareness flare in her eyes and the eager hunger that followed, he felt sure she'd make good on her promise.

He'd keep his promises, too, being as stubborn as his wife, and willing to fight for what he cared about. Above all else, he cared about Pru. He couldn't find the right words to express all the things stored up in his heart, but he had ways of communicating that were far better.

He pulled out a chair for her. "After dinner, we'll go for a walk and I'll show you some of my favorites."

Epilogue

On Sunday, Arch hitched up the wagon and took Pru into town to attend church. The streets of Centralia looked different on Sundays. Farmers traded their dusty denims for suits and those who were lucky enough to have wives paraded well-dressed women on their arms. Arch cast a proud look at his beaming bride.

Pru had put on the pretty calico dress she'd worn for their wedding and had done her hair in a style he favored, with soft curls framing her face. She hadn't taken note of his admiration because she was too busy looking at the folks on the sidewalk. "Is it me, or do you think people are staring at us?"

She wasn't imagining things. He'd noticed the curious stares, too.

Five days earlier, his brothers had been taken through a speedy trial. The judged had sentenced them to a month of hard labor and put them to work building a nice boarding house for single young ladies brought in by the railroad.

Poetic justice, Pru had called it. Arch dubbed it a

lucky break. His Ma insisted she could handle things for a month without his help, which meant he and Pru wouldn't have to give up their home or their dreams. But their troubles were far from over.

He winked at his wife. "They're looking at you and wishing they were me."

"Oh pshaw. If they're admiring anything, it's Sophie."

"She is a pretty horse. But she doesn't have a fancy straw hat."

Pru reached up and stroked one of the feathers. "It's a silly thing…useless, really. Doesn't provide more than a speck of shade."

"But it looks so nice perched on your head like that. Those are jealous looks you're getting from the other women."

A rosy stain appeared beneath his bride's cheekbones. "I very much doubt it, but I'm glad you're proud to be seen with me."

"I'd bust my buttons if I was any prouder." He loved lavishing praise on her, as much as he loved the way her skin glowed when he piled on the compliments.

Arch guided Sophie to an open spot at a hitching rail outside O'Shea's opera house. Like most businesses, it was closed on Sundays. Mr. O'Shea let the place be used for worship services, as the town didn't yet have a church building.

The crowd gathered on the sidewalk included Centralia's most influential citizens, some of whom had made it clear that he didn't belong here on Sunday, even though he was welcome in the place the other six days of the week.

Maybe it wasn't such a good idea to bring Pru to town so soon after the trial.

She had borne the brunt of the cruel gossip surrounding the case, and being associated with a *godless bootlegger* had stained her good name. He didn't care what folks thought about him, but he wanted everyone who doubted her morality to see that they were wrong about her. She deserved their respect and he would defend his wife's honor to the last breath.

He tugged at the knot on his tie. Pru had gushed about how nice he looked, and he suspected she knew he'd put on the formal suit that had belonged to his father in order to make a good impression for her sake. Even though dressing up like a gentleman wouldn't fool anybody into thinking he was one.

"Shall we go in?" she asked.

Earlier, she'd jumped at the chance to come to church. He didn't want her to think his reluctance had anything to do with her.

"It's been awhile since I darkened the door of a church."

"Then you have nothing to worry about. That's an opera house, not a church."

"True enough."

She squared her shoulders. "We have to do this, Arch. If we stay away like we're hiding, that will feed the malicious gossip about what happened."

He didn't hesitate another moment and hopped down. Her courage fortified his determination. He'd make these folks respect her, even if he had to force them to their knees. One good thing about having a mean reputation, it inspired fear. He hadn't worn the long knife he usually carried, but he didn't need a weapon to appear intimidating.

Prudence gripped her husband's arm. Not too tight, or he would pick up on her fear and take her home. He'd made this trip for her, knowing how much she wanted to reconnect with her friends. What he didn't know was that she wanted this for his sake even more than hers.

Thinking back, she realized she hadn't seen him around town because he remained on the fringes of society. That's where he thought he ought to be, and no one had ever told him different. He deserved better, and she would see to it that he was given the chance to become a respected member of the community. Even a leader, if that's what he wanted. His outgoing, friendly personality would draw people to him, once they got to know him.

Inside the opera house, the tables had been moved to one side. Chairs were arranged in rows in front of the stage where a podium had been set up. Heavy velvet curtains, a new addition, were drawn back from the windows and light flooded the room. The door had been propped open to let in more light and any breeze that might be found.

She halted at the back of the room. All but one or two single seats appeared to be occupied. A few people glanced over their shoulders and then turned around, pointedly ignoring them.

Prudence searched the crowd. Where were her friends? She'd anticipated seeing at least a few friendly faces.

Reverend Stillwater stepped up to the podium. He scanned the crowd, not really noticing them, and then looked down and appeared to be thumbing through his Bible, almost like he was nervous. He had arrived in town around the same time as the first trainload of brides. Being the only preacher, he'd been called on to perform marriages and recently had started the church. His skin looked darker inside the unlit room, shadows emphasizing sharp planes on a face that reminded her more of a devil than a saint.

Would he condemn them for daring to show up and loudly proclaim their need for repentance? That's what her father would've done. As much as she'd loved him and admired his strength of character, she knew in her heart he had been wrong to be so judgmental.

Arch leaned down and whispered. "Better pick a seat. The preacher's about to get started."

"Where? There aren't any together. No one's making room."

A woman in the front row wearing a frilly bonnet turned to look at them. Her eyes widened in surprise then filled with delight.

Hope Waverly. Thank heavens.

Her friend waved to them.

"She wants us to come up there," Arch pointed out.

The aisle between the chairs stretched out like a shadowy path through a dark forest. Prudence's heart quivered with an equal mixture of relief and dread. Arch placed his warm palm over the back of her hand and tucked her fingers more securely into the crook of his elbow.

A fearsome frown marred her husband's features. Good heavens. What had come over him? He'd been wearing a devastating smile before they entered the building.

Alarm flashed on the faces of curious onlookers. Women clung to their husbands' arms and gathered their children close.

"You look like an angry bear," Prudence whispered out of the side of her mouth. "Try not to scare them."

At last, they reached the front row.

Prudence's spirits plummeted. Beside Hope sat a squirming boy, Danny Braddock, and next to him, his mother Susannah. Mr. Hardt, the railroad agent, had his ankle crossed over his knee and his hat held loosely in his lap, seemingly oblivious to the woman sitting next to him. Susannah hugged a floral shawl like she was trying to keep out the cold. The temperature of the air felt like a hundred degrees.

One chair remained empty.

Susannah looked up. The tight strain on her face melted into profound relief. She turned to the man next to her and motioned with her hands, looked like she was shooing him.

No words were spoken, at least none Prudence could hear, but Mr. Hardt quickly vacated his seat. He gestured for her and Arch to take the two chairs, and then moved several rows back, finding a seat beside a grizzled settler, who eyed him with blatant disdain.

Prudence sat beside Susannah, stifling a laugh. Arch settled in next to her. His frown had vanished and a half smile tilted one side of his mouth.

She leaned toward her friend. "Thank you!"

"Thank *you*. I feared I would be forced to endure Mr. Hardt's presence throughout the entire service," Susannah said under her breath. She dropped her shawl over the back of the chair, apparently no longer feeling the need for warmth.

Prudence resisted the temptation to look behind her. "Don't you think it's odd that Mr. Hardt chose to sit next to you, knowing how you feel about him?" she whispered.

Susannah rolled her eyes. "He does it to torment me."

Somehow, it didn't fit that a man like Hardt, who had his hands full managing the railroad's business, would waste time taunting a woman. Unless... "Maybe he likes you."

"What a dreadful thought." The blush that stained Susannah's cheeks belied the claim that she found Mr. Hardt's attention *dreadful*. Possibly, quite the opposite.

Prudence kept her suspicions to herself. It seemed unlikely those two would work through their differences, considering they were equally intransigent. Then again, no one would've expected a Daughter of Temperance to fall in love with the local bootlegger...her least of all.

"Good morning everyone!" The preacher's greeting grabbed her attention. He looked directly at her with those piercing black eyes, and her skin prickled in response.

Oh no...

"Welcome, Mr. and Mrs. Childers," he said in a low voice, but loud enough for the others to hear. "It gladdens my heart to see you here. I'm sure everyone else feels the same way."

Her breath came out on a rush. God bless Reverend Stillwater. He had publicly accepted them, thus setting an example for others to follow.

He redirected his attention to the congregation. "Who would like to lead us in a hymn?"

Tomblike silence filled the room.

Prudence couldn't bear to look around and be wounded by the censure in people's eyes. She shouldn't have tried to force her way back into polite society, dragging Arch along to be humiliated, as well; and she'd made things worse for the preacher, who had been kind to them. She reached for Arch's hand. They would leave rather than bring trouble to this congregation.

Hope leapt to her feet. "I will, Reverend. I'll lead the singing."

A gasp of surprise came from Susannah. Prudence gaped in disbelief. They both knew that Hope suffered from painful shyness. She could be friendly and chatty among close friends, but she rarely spoke up in a group, much less in front of a crowd.

Hope didn't look around. Rather, she kept her eyes trained forward, seemingly fastened on the surprised gaze of the preacher. Her voice started soft, wavering, and then rose in volume and strength. The familiar hymn she chose fit perfectly with Reverend Stillwater's charitable remarks.

"Blest be the tie that binds
Our hearts in Christian love!
The fellowship of kindred minds
Is like to that above…"

Astonished, Prudence turned to meet Arch's eyes. He threaded their fingers together. They stood and joined in, singing. Her husband's rich, resonant baritone made a perfect accompaniment to Hope's pure soprano. Prudence pitched her voice to blend with the others and sang from the depths of her heart.

Susannah bolted to her feet, holding her son's hand. She took Prudence's free hand, as her son reached for Hope, who gathered his small fingers.

More voices joined them, a few at first, and then a great swell. Chairs scraped the wooden floor as people stood. They moved into the aisle, reaching across to their neighbors. The sweet song of unity wove them together and for one precious moment, they sang as one.

Tears welled and Prudence let them flow, unheeded. Her heart couldn't contain all the emotions she experienced in that moment. She and Arch would face challenges, of course. Not everyone would accept them. There were as many prejudiced, self-righteous saints as there were sinners. But for the moment, goodness had overcome.

After the service, she and Arch lagged behind to chat with friends. Charm and Patrick came up to greet them. Others offered best wishes as they filed past the front to greet the preacher. When the crowd thinned, Reverend Stillwater made his way over and shook hands with Arch. He greeted Prudence and thanked Hope for her gift. Hope beamed as if he had been the one to bestow it.

Oh dear. Hope, smitten with the preacher, who didn't have a penny to his name if the worn condition of his suit was any indication... This might prove to be difficult. The contract signed by the women who'd come out west to be brides specifically stated they had to marry a settler with a valid land claim. Hardhearted Mr. Hardt wouldn't make an exception.

"Prudence!"

The call came from amidst the departing crowd.

Delilah wormed her way through bodies headed in the opposite direction. Beautiful as always, with her black hair arranged to cover a minor flaw that she believed made her unlovable.

Prudence's heart ached for her friend. She knew what it was like to believe no one could ever love her.

"Oh my stars, how I've missed you! I'm sure you haven't had a minute to miss me, being newly married." Delilah gave her a hug and then turned to Arch, tipping her head to present the unmarred side of her face. Her gaze flicked over him, widening for a split second before she regained her perfect comportment. "Good day to you, Mr. Childers."

Arch sketched a very gentlemanly bow. "And to you, Miss Bodean."

Being a polite Southern lady, Delilah didn't outright express her surprise, but she had to be startled by the change. When she'd met Arch, at the spur-of-the-moment wedding, he hadn't been at his best—beat up, dazed, wearing a borrowed shirt and filthy trousers.

Delilah leaned closer to Prudence, with a twinkle in her eyes. "Why, I do declare, he's quite the catch."

Prudence hugged her husband's arm, proudly. "He is indeed."

"Don't let her fool you. It took some mighty hard convincing on my part."

"How did you convince her?" Delilah asked.

A wicked gleam sparked in Arch's eyes. He'd better not go into the specifics of how he'd convinced her.

Prudence elbowed her husband and whispered, "Remember, we're in church."

"You told me it was an opera house," he returned under his breath.

The rascal.

She supplied a more suitable answer than what would be on the tip of his tongue. "I came to realize we were well suited."

Arch gave a soft snort. "Now Pru, you're in a church, remember? No lying."

She didn't think God would mind her discretion. However, Arch would provide a truthful answer if she didn't. Prudence lowered her voice so only Delilah could hear. "The truth? He was a temptation I couldn't resist."

The End.

Also by E.E. Burke

The Bride Train Series

VALENTINE'S ROSE, BOOK 1

PATRICK'S CHARM, BOOK 2

American Mail-Order Brides Series

VICTORIA, BRIDE OF KANSAS

SANTA'S MAIL-ORDER BRIDE

Steam! Romance and Rails Series

KATE'S OUTLAW

HER BODYGUARD

A DANGEROUS PASSION

FUGITIVE HEARTS

www.eeburke.com

To learn about upcoming and new releases, please join
my newsletter:
https://www.eeburke.com/news.html

E.E. Burke is an award-winning author of sensual, humorous, heartfelt historical romance. Her latest series, *The Bride Train*, features a cast of unusual characters thrown together through a misguided bride lottery.

Her books have topped Amazon bestseller lists and her writing has earned accolades in regional and national contests, including the RWA's prestigious Golden Heart®.

Over the years, she's been a disc jockey, a journalist and an advertising executive, before finally getting around to living the dream—writing stories readers can get lost in.

You can read more about E.E. at www.eeburke.com.

Good
Intentions

A DragonEye, PI Novella

Karina Fabian

Laser Cow Press

MERRITT ISLAND, FL

Laser Cow Press
Merritt Island, FL
https://fabianspace.com

Publisher's Note: This is a work of fiction. Names, characters, places, and incidents are a product of the author's imagination. Locales and public names are sometimes used for atmospheric purposes. Any resemblance to actual people, living or dead, or to businesses, companies, events, institutions, or locales is completely coincidental.

Cover art by Dawn Grimes
DragonEye Logo by Len Fabian

Book Layout © 2017 BookDesignTemplates.com

Good Intentions/Karina Fabian -- 1st ed.
ISBN 978-1-956489-12-5